Jake saw a ra__ flicker across Allison's face.

Disappointment, worry, relief. He latched on to the last one. She wanted him gone.

Then why was she here? Why did she insist on pushing past his caution when absolutely nothing good could come of it?

Jake wished for the thousandth time he could erase one terrible day from their lives. He was comfortable with Allison, *liked* her, a dangerous thing, then and now. She made him smile. She even made him believe in himself. Or she once had. With everything in him he wanted to know this grown-up Allison, a dangerous, troubling proposition.

"You've grown up." Stupid thing to say, but better than yanking her into his arms.

She tilted her head, smile quizzical. "Is that a good thing or a bad thing?"

For him? Very bad.

Allison had definitely grown up.

And Jake Hamilton was in major trouble.

Books by Linda Goodnight

Love Inspired

LINDA GOODNIGHT

New York Times bestselling author and winner of a RITA® Award for excellence in inspirational fiction, Linda Goodnight has also won a Booksellers' Best Award, an ACFW Book of the Year Award and a Reviewers' Choice Award from *RT Book Reviews*. Linda has appeared on the Christian bestseller list, and her romance novels have been translated into more than a dozen languages. Active in orphan ministry, this former nurse and teacher enjoys writing fiction that carries a message of hope and light in a sometimes dark world. She and her husband live in Oklahoma. Visit her website, www.lindagoodnight.com. To browse a current listing of Linda Goodnight's titles, please visit www.Harlequin.com.

Cowboy Under
the Mistletoe

New York Times Bestselling Author
Linda Goodnight

Recycling programs
for this product may
not exist in your area.

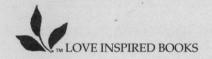

ISBN-13: 978-0-373-87921-2

Cowboy Under the Mistletoe

Copyright © 2014 by Linda Goodnight

www.Harlequin.com

Printed in U.S.A.

Now, however, it is time to forgive and comfort him.
Otherwise he may be overcome by discouragement.
—*2 Corinthians* 2:7

Chapter One

Someone was at the Hamilton house. Someone in a black pickup truck bearing a bull rider silhouette on the back window.

Curious, with a tremor in her memory, Allison Buchanon pulled her Camaro sports car to the stop sign in a quiet neighborhood of Gabriel's Crossing, Texas, and sat for a moment pondering the anomaly. She drove past this corner at least once a week on her way to her best friend's home. She hadn't seen any sign of life in the rambling old house for a long while. Not since before Grandmother Hamilton fell and broke her hip several months ago. And Jake had been gone so long no one even cursed his name anymore.

If Allison had a funny quiver in her stomach, she played it off as anticipation of Faith's bridal shower this afternoon. As hostess, she wanted to arrive early and make sure everything—including her dearest friend—was perfect.

She glanced at the dash clock. Three hours early might be overkill.

On the opposite corner, Dakota Weeks and a half-dozen fat puppies rolled around in the fading grass while the mama dog wagged her tail and smiled proudly, occasionally poking her nose into the ten-year-old boy's hand for a head rub. Allison grinned and waved.

A boy and his dogs on Saturday afternoon put her in mind of her older brothers. Even now as adults, rolling in the grass with a dog—or each other if a football game broke out—was a common occurrence. And today was a perfect day to be outside. The weather was that cusp season when cool breezes crowded out the scent of mowed grass, Dads cleaned out chimneys and Moms stored away the shorts and swimsuits. Or as townsfolk would say, "football weather."

Like many small Texas towns, Gabriel's Crossing lived and breathed high school football year round, but especially in the fall. Teenage boys in pads and helmets became heroes, not only on Friday night but every day. Golden boys. Boys of the gridiron.

Exactly the reason Jake Hamilton was no longer welcome at her mother's table or a lot of other places in Gabriel's Crossing.

Oh, but they didn't know the Jake Allison had known. The Jake who carried her darkest, most humiliating secret, the one she'd never shared with another living soul.

Casting one last worried glance toward the Hamilton house, Allison convinced herself the truck belonged to a lawn service or maybe some long-lost relative looking to take over the place, not Jake Hamilton.

She eased her foot off the brake and started across the intersection. The front door to the house opened and a man walked out onto the small concrete porch.

This time Allison's stomach did more than quiver. It fell to the floorboard and took her breath with it.

Jake.

She slammed on the brake and stared. It was him all right. Trim and tight muscled in fitted Wranglers, dusty boots and black cowboy hat, he looked as dangerously handsome as ever.

His head turned her direction, and Allison realized she'd stopped at midintersection. She started forward again. At the last possible second, the steering wheel seemed to take on a life of its own because the Camaro swung into the Hamilton driveway and came to a stop.

With the spontaneity her parents considered impulsive, Allison hopped out of the running car and walked right up to the man, her pulse in overdrive.

"Hello, Jake. Long time." Funny how normal her voice sounded even when she stared into fathomless olive green eyes with lashes as black as midnight.

He hadn't changed much except for a new scar below one eye, and she fought off the crazy urge to soothe it with a touch the way she'd once soothed his football bumps and bruises. He'd also grown facial hair in the form of a very short, scant mustache above a bit of scruff, and his side-burns were long. She couldn't decide if she liked the look but then, when had Jake Hamilton cared one whit about what anyone else thought? Especially a Buchanon.

"You shouldn't be here, Allison." His voice was the same, a low note, surprisingly soft but steel edged as if to drive her away. The way he'd done before.

"We're adults now. We can be anywhere we choose."

Jutting one hip, he tipped his hat with a thumb. His nostrils flared. "Ya think?"

"You owe me a dance."

The reminder must have caught him off guard. Something flickered in his eyes, a brief flame of memory and pleasure that died just as quickly unborn.

Jaw hard as flint, he said, "Better run home, little girl, before the big bad wolf gets you."

Before she could tell him that nothing he'd ever done would change what she knew that no other Buchanon understood, Jake spun away from her and slammed inside the house, leaving her standing in the front yard. Alone and embarrassed. Exactly like before.

* * *

He had as much right to be in this town as the Buchanons. Maybe more. His great-great-something on his daddy's side had founded Gabriel's Crossing back in the mid-1800s when Texas was a whole other country and the adjacent hills of Oklahoma were wilder than any bull he'd thrown his rope over.

Jake banged his fist against the countertop of his family home. Right or not, being here would not be easy. Nearly broke, he needed to be working, and if that wasn't enough to move him on, the Buchanon brothers were. And Allison. Especially Allison.

But Granny Pat was his only living relative. Anyway, the only one that claimed him. She'd been his anchor most of his life, but now the tables had turned. She needed him, and he wouldn't fail her, no matter how hard the weeks and months ahead.

He'd wanted her to give up the Hamilton house to live with him in his trailer in Stephenville, but she'd wanted to come home. Home to Gabriel's Crossing and the familiar old house that had been in the Hamilton family since statehood. He understood, at least in part. There was history here, joy and sorrow. He'd tasted both.

Granny Pat had raised him single-handedly in this house after his daddy died and his mother ran off. Grandpa was here, too, his grandmother claimed, and though her husband had been dead for longer than Jake had been alive, she missed him. Ralph, according to Granny Pat, had never liked hospitals and hadn't visited her in the convalescent center one single time.

As if that wasn't scary enough, who was the first familiar face Jake had to see in Gabriel's Crossing? Allison Buchanon. His heart crumpled in his chest like a wad of paper tossed into a fire pit, withering to black ashes. Allison of the dark fluffy hair and warm brown eyes. She'd always seen more in him than anyone else had, especially her family. Foolish girl.

Although as small as a child, Allison could hammer a nail as easily as she could back-flip from a cheerleading pyramid, an action that had sent his teenage chest soaring and turned his mouth dry as dust. And she'd broken that same young man's heart with one sentence. *My family would kill me if they saw us together.*

No, he'd said, *they'd kill me.* They'd have had every right, after what he'd done.

The rodeo circuit attracted plenty of buckle bunnies and if a man was so inclined, he could have a new girl every night. With everything in him, Jake wanted to put Allison and her family behind him, but he never had. They mattered, and the wrong he'd done lay on his shoulders, an elephant-size guilt. No matter what Allison said, he'd never been anyone's hero.

When he'd been a lonely boy living with his grandma, the Buchanons had been his dream family, a mom and dad, brothers and sisters. A boy with none of those yearned for the impossible. For a while, for those years when Quinn had been his best friend and Allison had thought he was the moon, he'd basked in the Buchanon glow.

Allison. Why had she pulled into the driveway? And why had he been so glad to see her? Didn't she remember the trouble they'd caused? That *he'd* caused?

He rubbed a hand over the thick dust coating the counters, coating everything in the musty old house with the pink siding and dark paneling.

He should have stuck to the rodeo circuit and stayed away from Gabriel's Crossing for another nine or ninety years, but sometimes life didn't give you choices. Four years ago, when he'd handed the reins to Jesus at a cowboy church in Cheyenne, he'd vowed to do the right thing from that moment on, no matter how much it hurt. Coming home to help Granny Pat was the right thing. And boy, did it hurt.

He didn't have enough money or time to be here. He needed to make every rodeo he could before the season ended, but Granny Pat came first. He'd figure out the rest. Somehow.

Once his grandma was up and going, he'd get out of Dodge before trouble—in the form of a Buchanon—found him again.

No one in their right minds had seven kids these days. Which said a lot about her mother and father.

The next afternoon, Allison pushed open the front door to her parents' rambling split-level house on Barley Street and marched in without knocking. Nobody would have heard her anyway over the noise in the living room. The TV blared football between the Cowboys and the Giants while her dad and four brothers yelled at the quarterback and each other in the good-natured, competitive spirit of the Buchanon clan. Her stick-skinny younger sister Jayla was right with them, getting in her two cents about the lousy play calling by the offensive coordinator while Charity, the oldest and only married sibling, doled out peanut butter and jelly sandwiches to her two kids.

"Home sweet home." Allison stepped over a sprawled Dawson whose long legs seemed to stretch from the bottom of the couch halfway across the room.

"Hey, sis," Dimpled Dawson, twin to Sawyer, offered an absentminded fist bump before yelling. "You missed the block, you moron!"

"I'll do better next time," Allison said, pretending not to understand. Dawson ignored that, too.

"Where's Mom?"

"Somewhere."

Brothers could be so helpful.

"Jayla?" she implored of her sister, who was scrunched on the dirt-brown sofa between Sawyer and Quinn.

Jayla, twisting the ends of her flaxen hair into tight, nervous corkscrews, never took her eyes off the game. She lifted a finger and pointed. "Backyard."

Backyard. That figured. Mom would rather putter in her flowers, though she'd wander in and out of the huge Buchanon-built house simply to spend time with her kids.

Before Allison made the turn into the kitchen, Brady snagged her wrist. Like Dawson, he was on the floor but propped against the wall with his dog sprawled across his lap. Dawg, a shaggy mix of shepherd, lab and who-knew-what, raised a bushy eyebrow in her direction, but otherwise, like the siblings, didn't budge.

"Aren't you going to watch the game?"

Allison's nerves jittered. Some things were more important than the game, although she would not share this minority opinion with any relative in the large, overcrowded living room.

"Later."

He tilted his head to one side, a flash of curiosity in his startling cerulean eyes. Brady, her giant Celtic warrior brother who bore minimal resemblance to the rest of the Buchanons. "Everything okay, Al?"

Jake Hamilton, one hip slung low as a gunslinger, imposed on her mental viewer. "Sure."

"Touchdown Cowboys!" someone shouted, and the room erupted in high fives and victory dances. His curiosity forgotten, Brady leaped to his feet and swirled her around in a two-step, as light on his feet as when he'd been chasing quarterbacks at Texas Tech. Allison, regardless of the worry, couldn't help but laugh. Her brothers were crazy wonderful, her protectors and friends, the shoulders she could always cry on, except that one awful night when she hadn't dared. Her heart swelled with love. What would she do without them? And how would they react when they learned Jake Hamilton was back in town?

Brady planted a loud smack on her cheek and turned her loose. Before he could ask any more prying questions, she high-fived her way through the elated sea of bodies and headed toward the kitchen. There she grabbed a bag of tortilla chips, one of several that yawned open on the counter next to upturned lids coated with various dips.

Allison skirted the long table for ten that centered the family kitchen-dining room to push open the patio doors and stepped out onto the round rock stepping stones installed by her brothers.

The yard was a green oasis, a retreat in the middle of a neighborhood of long time friends, of dogs that wandered and of kids that tended to do the same.

Karen Buchanon, matriarch of the rowdy Buchanon clan, looked up from repotting a sunny yellow chrysanthemum. At fifty-nine, she looked good in jean capris and a red blouse, her blond hair pulled back at the nape, her figure thicker but still shapely.

"There you are," Mom said. "You missed the first quarter. Are you hungry?"

Allison lifted the bag of chips. "Got it covered."

"Not very substantial." Her mother laid aside a well-worn trowel, pushed to a stand and stripped off her green gardening gloves. "That should brighten up the backyard."

"Mums are so pretty this time of year."

"Why aren't you watching the game?"

Allison crunched another salty chip. Her mother knew her too well to believe she'd abandoned a Cowboys game to talk about mums. Mom was the gardener whose skills served the Buchanon Construction Company. Allison barely knew a mum from an oak tree. Accounts payable was her area of expertise, such as it was, though Dawson often said, and she agreed, that Allison preferred all things wedding to construction.

But the family business was too important, too ingrained in her DNA to abandon in pursuit of some fantasy. Grandpa and Grandma Buchanon had built Buchanon Construction from the ground up before turning the business over to their only son—her dad. All seven Buchanon kids had known from the time they were big enough to toddle around in Dad's hard hat that they were destined to build houses, to provide beautiful homes for families. Building was not only the Buchanon way, it was their calling.

But construction was not on her mind at the moment. Not even close. "I have something to tell you. Something important."

Mom's eyes narrowed in speculation. Even in shadow from the enormous old silver maple that shaded the back yard, Allison could see the wheels turning. Her mother sat down in the green-striped-canopy swing and patted the seat. "Come here. Might as well get it out. You've been stewing."

"How do you always know?"

Her mom pointed. "That little muscle between your eyebrows gives you up every time."

Allison touched the spot.

She had been stewing. Since the moment Jake turned his back and walked away, a dark worry had flown in and now hovered like a vulture over a cow carcass. She'd told Faith, of course. Except for that one shuddery secret she never spoke of, she told her best friend since first grade everything. She'd even cried on Faith's shoulder years ago when Jake had packed a weathered old pickup and left for good.

Allison gnawed on her bottom lip. She was over him. At least, she'd told herself as much for the past few years. But she remembered, too, the terrible injustice done to a heartbroken boy.

Mom would find out anyway sooner or later. The whole family would. Then the mud would hit the fan.

She averted her gaze, watched a blue butterfly kiss a lavender aster.

"Mama," she said. "Jake's back in town."

For a full minute, the only sound was the bee-buzz of hummingbirds and the faint football noise from inside the house. Down the street someone fired up a lawn mower.

Allison could feel the blood surging in her veins—hot and anxious and so terribly sorry. Not for her family. For Jake. That was the problem, as the family, especially her brothers, saw it. Allison was a traitor to the Buchanon name. Back when the pain was rawest for everyone, she'd sided with Jake. They hadn't understood her loyalty. And if she had shared her secret, that singular defining reason for remaining loyal to Jake Hamilton, she would have caused an explosion of a different sort.

"Jake Hamilton?" her mother finally asked, voice tight.

The tone made Allison ache. "I saw him yesterday at the Hamilton house on my way to Faith's bridal shower."

"Why have you waited until now to tell me?"

"I stayed late at Faith's and then church this morning..." She lifted her palms, let them down again. In truth, she'd been a coward, putting off the inevitable unpleasant re-action and the feeling of betrayal that came along for the ride. "Faith said his grandma is coming home from the rehab center."

"Oh, Allison." Mom's tone was heavy-hearted. "The boys will be upset."

That was putting it mildly.

The *boys*. On the subject of Jake Hamilton, her sensible, caring, adult brothers behaved like children on a playground, the reason no one, even Quinn, had mentioned Jake in a very long time.

Mama pushed up from the swing and ran a hand over her mouth, a worry gesture Allison knew well. Karen Buchanon was the kindest heart in Gabriel's Crossing. She drove shut-ins to doctors' offices and sat up all night with the sick. She provided Christmas for needy families and fed stray dogs, but her children's needs came first. Always.

"That was so long ago. My brothers are grown men now. Isn't it time to forgive and forget?"

"Some things go too deep, honey. I wish we could put all of that behind us—" she clasped her hands together and gazed toward the back door as if she could see her children inside "—but wishing doesn't change anything. Jake did what he did, and Quinn suffered for it. Still suffers and always will."

"I know, Mama, and I hate what happened to Quinn as much as anyone. But Jake was seventeen. A boy. Teenagers do stupid things." She, of all people, understood how one stupid decision could be catastrophic.

She went to her mother's side, desperately wishing to tell everything about that one night at the river. But danger lurked in revelation and she didn't. She and Jake had a made a pact, a decision to protect the innocent as well as the guilty. "I'm not asking them to be his best friend, but we're supposed to be Christians. The holidays are coming up soon, the time for forgiveness and peace. Don't you think the boys could find it in their hearts to forgive Jake and move on? Couldn't we all?"

But Mama was already shaking her head. "Don't do this, honey. Stirring up the past will only cause hurt and trouble. Jake may be back in town—and I pray his visit is short—but for everyone's sake please don't get involved with him again."

Allison thought of the young Jake she'd known in grade school, though he'd been a whole year older and more mature, at least in her adoring eyes. Jake had been Quinn's best friend, a nice boy with sad eyes and a needy heart. The first boy she'd ever kissed. The one who lingered in her heart and memory even now.

Then she thought of Quinn. Her moody, broody brother. Her blood. Buchanon blood. And blood always won.

So she gave Mama the only possible answer. "All right."

But with sorrow born of experience, Allison knew this was one promise she wouldn't keep.

Chapter Two

He'd rather tangle with the meanest bull in the pasture than try to drive a wheelchair.

Jake yanked the folded bunch of canvas and metal from the bed of the pickup and shook it.

"How is this thing supposed to work anyway?" he said to exactly nobody.

Metal rattled against metal but the chair didn't open. He wished he'd paid more attention when the nurse—a puny little ninety-pound woman no bigger than Allison—folded the chair and tossed it into the back of his truck with ease. Getting the thing open and functioning couldn't be that difficult.

A hot summer sun roasted the back of his neck while Granny Pat waited patiently inside the cab with the AC running. She wasn't happy because he'd driven the truck right up next to the porch. She had fussed and complained that he'd leave ruts *with those massive tires* and ruin her yard. As if that wasn't enough, she'd been telling all this to Grandpa, a man who'd been dead for twenty years.

Jake's day had been lousy, and his head hurt. Last night, he'd barely slept after the meeting with Allison. He kept seeing her smile, her bounce, her determined kindness.

He didn't want to remember how much he'd missed her.

Then today, he'd made the trip to the convalescent center, a place that would depress Mary Poppins. If that and Granny's running conversations with Grandpa weren't enough to make his head pound, he'd stopped at Gabriel's Crossing Pharmacy to fill an endless number of prescriptions, and who should he see crossing the street? Brady Buchanon. Big, hot-tempered Brady.

Seeing a Buchanon brother was inevitable, but he planned to put off the moment as long as possible. So like a shamefaced secret agent, he'd pulled his hat low and hustled inside the drugstore before Brady caught a glimpse of him.

He hated feeling like an outcast, like the nasty fly in the pleasant soup of Gabriel's Crossing, but he was here, at least through the holidays, and the Buchanons would have to deal with it. So would everyone else who remembered the golden opportunity Jake had stolen from Quinn Buchanon and this small town with big dreams.

Then why did he feel like a criminal in his own hometown?

Granny Pat popped open the truck door and leaned out, her white hair as poufy as cotton candy. "Grandpa wants to know if you need help?"

Jake rolled his eyes heavenward. The sun nearly blinded him. "Be right there, Granny. Don't fall out."

At under five feet and shrinking, Granny Pat didn't have the strength to pull the heavy truck door closed and it edged further and further open. She was slowly being stretched from the cab.

Jake dropped the wheelchair and sprinted to her side, catching her a second before she tumbled out onto the grass. "Easy there. That door is heavy."

"I know it!" Fragile or not, she was still spit-and-vinegar Pat and clearly aggravated at her weakness. "I'm useless. Makes me so mad."

"Let's get you in the house. You'll feel better there."

"Get my wheelchair."

"The chair can wait." Forever as far as he was concerned.

With an ease that made him sad, Jake lifted his grandmother from the seat and carried her inside the house.

"Where to, madame?" he teased, though his heart ached. Granny Pat had been his mama, his daddy and his home all rolled into one strong, vital woman. She'd endured his wild teenage years and the scandal he'd caused that rocked Gabriel's Crossing. For her body to fail all because of one broken bone was unfair.

But when had life ever been fair?

"Put me in the recliner." She pointed toward one of two recliners in the living room—the blue one with a yellow-and-orange afghan tossed across the back.

He did as she asked.

Granny Pat tilted her head against the plush corduroy and gazed around the room with pleasure. "It's good to finally be home. I'll get my strength back here."

Her pleasure erased the sorrow of seeing Brady Buchanon and the nagging worry over finances. Granny Pat needed this, needed him, and he'd find a way to deal with the Buchanons and his empty pockets.

"You want some water or anything before I unload the truck?"

"Nothing but fresh air. Open some windows, Jacob. This house stinks. I don't know how you slept here in this must and dust."

As he threw open windows, Jake noticed the dirt and dead insects piled on the windowsills. "Maybe I can find a housekeeper?" His wallet would scream, but he'd figure out a way.

"I don't want some stranger in my house poking around."

"Nobody's a stranger in Gabriel's Crossing, Granny."

"Grandpa says something will turn up. Don't worry."

A bit of breeze drifted through the window, stirring dust in the sunlight.

"Granny Pat, you know Grandpa—"

"Yes, Jacob, I know." Her tone was patient as if he was the one with the mental lapses. "Now go on and bring in my belongings. I want my Sudoku book."

Jake jogged out to the truck, eyeing the pain-in-the-neck wheelchair he'd left against the back bumper. Granny Pat needed wheels to be mobile, and as much as he wanted to haul the chair to the nearest landfill, he was a man and he was determined to make the thing work.

He was wrestling the wheels apart when a Camaro rumbled to the stop sign on the corner. Precisely what he did not need. Allison Buchanon. He refused to look in her direction, hoping she'd roll on down the street. She didn't.

Allison, tenacious as a terrier, rolled down her window. "Having trouble?"

He looked up and his stomach tumbled down into his boots. The soft brown eyes he'd never forgotten snagged his. A sizzle of connection raised the hairs on his arms. "No."

Go away.

As if he wasn't the least interested in the wheelchair, he leaned the contraption against the truck and reached inside the bed for one of Granny Pat's suitcases.

The Camaro engine still rumbled next to the curb. Why didn't she mosey on down the road?

"You can't fool me," she hollered. "I remember."

And that was nearly his undoing. He could never fool Allison. No matter what he said or how hard he tried to pretend not to care that he was the town pariah, Allison saw through him. She'd even called him her hero.

"Go home, Allison." He didn't want her to remember any more than he wanted her feeling sorry for him.

She gunned the engine but instead of leaving, she pulled into the driveway and hopped out.

Hands deep in her back jeans pockets, she wore a sweater the color of a pumpkin that set off her dark hair. He didn't want to notice the changes in her, from the sweet-faced teenager to a beautiful woman, but he'd have to be dead not to.

Her fluffy, flyaway hair bounced as she approached the truck, took hold of the wheelchair and attempted to open it. When the chair didn't budge, she scowled. "What's wrong with this?"

Determined not to be friendly, Jake hefted a suitcase in each hand and started toward the house. He was here in Gabriel's Crossing because of Granny Pat. No other reason. Allison Buchanon didn't affect him in the least.

And bulls could fly.

Something pinged him in the back. A pebble thudded to the grass at his feet. He spun around. "Hey! Did you just hit me with a rock?"

She gave him a grin that was anything but friendly. "I figured out what's wrong with the chair."

He dropped the suitcases. "You did?"

"Come here and see for yourself. Unless you're scared of a girl."

He was scared of her all right. Allison Buchanon had the power to hurt him—or cause him to hurt himself. But intrigued by her claim, he went back to the chair.

A car chugged by the intersection going in the opposite direction. Across the street a dog barked, and down the block, some guy mowed his lawn, shooting the grassy smell all over the neighborhood. Normal activities in Gabriel's Crossing, though there was nothing normal about him standing in Granny Pat's yard with a Buchanon.

Man, his death wish must be worse than most.

He crossed his arms over his chest, careful not to get close enough to touch her. He didn't need reminders of her soft skin and flowery scent. "What?"

She went into a crouch, one hand holding up the chair. Her shoes were open toed and someone had painted her toenails orange and green like tiny pumpkins.

"That piece is bent and caught on the gear. See?"

He had no choice but to crouch beside her. There it was. Her sweet scent. Honeysuckle, he thought. Exactly the same as she'd worn in high school. Sweet and clean and pure.

Jake cleared his throat and gripped the chair. He needed to get a grip, all right.

"I got it," he said, thinking she'd leave now. She didn't.

He reached in and straightened the metal piece with his fingers, using more effort than he'd expected. A deep rut whitened along his index finger.

"Pliers would have been easier," she said. Then she grabbed the oversize wheels and popped open the stubborn wheelchair. "There. Ready to roll."

Jake stepped around to take the handles. Allison climbed up on the truck bumper and started unloading Granny Pat's belongings.

"I can get those."

"I came to see Miss Pat." She handed him a plastic sack of clothes. Granny had collected a dozen shopping bags filled with clothes along with her suitcases and medical supplies. Where a woman in a convalescent center acquired so much remained a puzzle. But then, women in general were a puzzle to most of the male species and Jake was no exception.

"You shouldn't have come."

"Let her be the judge of that."

"You know what I mean, Allison. Don't be mule-headed."

She hopped off the bumper, plopped a bag of plastic medical supplies into the wheelchair and went back for another. When he saw she wasn't leaving no matter what he said, he joined her, unloading the items, much of which fit in the wheelchair.

"So, how have you been?" she asked, her tone all spunky and cute as if no bad blood ran between her brothers and him.

"Good."

"What does that mean?"

He squinted at her over the tailgate. "You're not going to give up, are you?"

"We were friends once, Jake. I believe in second chances."

Friends? Yes, they'd been friends, but toward the end, he'd been falling in love with his best friend's sister.

He shook off the random thought. Whatever had been budding between two teenagers was long dead and buried.

"How's Quinn?"

He hadn't meant to ask, hadn't intended to open that door, but he held his breath, praying for something he couldn't name.

"He's the architect for Buchanon Construction now."

"Granny Pat told me he went to Tech with Brady." He didn't say the other; that Quinn's full-ride football scholarship had disappeared on a bloody October morning. "Does he ever talk about—"

"No, and I don't want to either." She glanced away, toward a pair of puppies galloping around the neighbor's front yard, her eyebrows drawn together in a worried frown. "Quinn has a decent life here in Gabriel's Crossing. Maybe the path wasn't the one he'd expected to take, but he survived."

Jake slowly exhaled. "That's good. Real good."

Quinn was okay. The accident happened long ago. Maybe Jake was no longer the hated pariah. People moved on. Everyone except him and he'd been stuck in the past so long, he didn't know how to move off high-center. "What about you? Why aren't you married with a house full of kids?"

He hadn't meant to ask that either.

She shrugged. The pumpkin sweater bunched up around her white neck. "I've had my chances."

He was sure she had, and he wondered why she hadn't taken them. "Still working for your dad?"

"In the offices with Jayla."

"Little sister grew up?"

"We all do, Jake." She smiled a little. "I keep the books, do payroll, billing. All the fun numbers stuff."

"Put that high school accounting award to good use, didn't you?"

Her eyes crinkled at the corners. "You remember that?"

He remembered everything about her, his cheerleader and champion when life had been too difficult to live. "Hard to forget. You wore that medal around your neck for months."

"Fun times."

Yes, they were. Before he'd destroyed everything with one stupid decision.

"Faith's getting married," she said.

Faith Evans, her sidekick. The long and the short, as the guys had called them. Faith had grown to nearly six feet tall by sixth grade, and Allison had barely been tall enough to reach the gas pedal when she'd turned sixteen. "Yeah? Who's the lucky guy?"

"They met in college. Derrick Cantelli. I'm coordinating her wedding." She tilted back on the heels of her sandals, her warm brown eyes searching his. "Granny Pat told me you live in Stephenville now."

"Land of the rodeo cowboys."

"Do you like it there?"

"Sure." He glanced away, afraid she'd read the truth in his eyes. "We better get this in the house before Granny Pat starts hollering."

He gave the wheels a nudge with his boot.

"Unlock it," Allison said.

"It has a lock?" He poked around and found the lever, released the device with a snap, and incredibly, the chair rolled a few inches. "How did you know that?"

"Brady had knee surgery his last year at Tech."

Just that quick, the elephant was back in the room. "I watched him play on TV a few times. He was good."

But not as good as Quinn. No one in the state had been as good at football as Quinn Buchanon. Quinn, with the golden arm that had turned to blood.

He gave the wheelchair a shove and rolled toward the front door.

He'd gone quiet on her again. When Allison thought they'd moved past that awkward stage, past his determination to be the rude, don't-care cowboy, he had clammed up again. Between his reluctance and her brothers' animosity, she wondered why she kept trying.

But she knew why. Though she was a Buchanon with every cell in her body, her brothers were wrong to hold a grudge. Anger would not restore Quinn's arm to normal.

Anger would not regain his chance at an NFL career. All bitterness had ever done was make them miserable.

Like now. If they knew she was here, her brothers would have a fit. Just as they would have a fit if they'd known about the other thing. They'd have done something crazy.

But she was as drawn to Jake Hamilton today as she had been in high school. He was her buddy, her first love, and foolish though she might be, she yearned to help him, to be his friend again, to repay a debt of love and loyalty.

If he'd revealed her secret nine years ago, maybe her family wouldn't despise Jake so much. But he'd kept silent because she had begged him to. And he'd suffered for his loyalty.

He could walk off and leave her in the yard every time she visited, but she wouldn't stop trying. He meant too much to her.

If that was pathetic, so be it.

Grabbing a small black suitcase Jake had left behind, she followed him into the house. Her stomach sank like a brick in a pond when she spotted Miss Pat in the big blue corduroy recliner. The once vital, high-energy woman had shriveled to child-size in the months since her hip surgery. She looked a hundred instead of in her early seventies.

"Hi, Miss Pat."

"Look here, Ralph, it's little Allison. Isn't she pretty as a picture?"

Ralph? Who was Ralph? She looked to Jake for help but he'd moved around behind his grandmother and simply shook his head at her. Allison got the message and didn't press the subject.

She pulled a worn leather ottoman close to the recliner and plopped down. "How you feeling, Miss Pat? Can I do anything for you?"

"You sure can, sweetie. I am useless as a newborn." Her

strong voice didn't match her body. "Get my purse over there on the table where Jacob stuck it, and then find my Sudoku book in all that mess of sacks."

"I can do that." Allison hopped up, amused but pleased that Miss Pat's personality hadn't faded like her body, a good sign she had the grit to stage a fourth quarter comeback. "Would you like for me to unpack and put everything away? I'd be pleased to do it."

"Now, there's a fine idea. See, Jacob." She tilted her head back to gaze up at her grandson. "Your grandpa said something would turn up and here she is. Allison will help get this place in order. Won't you, Allison?"

"Well, sure I will, if that's what you need."

"Good. This house needs a cleaning from top to bottom."

"I can do that." Never mind that her brothers would go ballistic to know she was in the Hamilton house with Jake. She was here for Miss Pat. Helping a friend was the Buchanon way. And yes, she admitted, she wanted to get to know Jake again. He was a memory that wouldn't go away. "I can't tonight, but I'll come by tomorrow after work. How's that sound?"

"She's a jewel, isn't she, Jacob? Just like in high school when she was sweet on you."

Jake looked as if he'd swallowed a bug. Allison's face heated, but she grinned. Miss Pat never minced words.

"Come on, *Jacob*," she said, teasing him about the seldom-used name. "Help me find that puzzle book."

Reluctantly, and with his expression shuttered, he started crinkling plastic sacks. Allison fetched the handbag, handed it off to Miss Pat and joined Jake in the hunt for that all-important puzzle book.

Each time she looked up, their eyes met. Every bit as quickly, one of them would look away. She was acutely aware of his masculine presence, his cowboy swagger, his manly, outdoors scent. Aware in a way that disturbed her thinking.

She found the thick Sudoku pad in the bottom of an ugly brown plastic washbasin.

"Here's your puzzle book, Miss Pat. Need a pencil?"

"Got one in my purse." Miss Pat had already extracted a cell phone and was scrolling the contacts. "No, Ralph, it's not time for my meds."

Jake glanced at a square wall clock hanging next to an outdated calendar, a sad reminder that no one had lived here for several months. "Another hour, Granny."

"That's what I told Ralph. I've got to text Mae at the prison and let her know I survived the ride home."

Jake rolled his eyes. "Carson Convalescence was not a prison."

"A lot you'd know about it." Using an index finger, she tapped a message on the phone's keyboard. "Ah, there we go. Poor Mae. Stuck in that prison through Christmas."

With a resigned shake of his head, Jake grabbed two suitcases and lugged them through a doorway. Allison followed with an armful of crinkling Walmart sacks.

"Do you know where everything goes?" she asked.

"No."

"We'll figure it out." Allison opened the closet and took out some empty hangers and then started unpacking the mishmash of belongings.

Jake edged around her, looking uncertain and a little thunderous. "You don't have to do this."

"Yes, I do."

"Why?" He paused in hanging up a dress to stare at her across Miss Pat's dusty dresser.

Every nerve ending reacted to that green gaze, but Allison refused to let her jumbled feelings show. "Because Ralph said I would."

He grinned. Finally. He had a killer grin beneath olive eyes that had driven more than one girl to doodle his name on the edge of her spiral notebook. Including Allison. But that was in high school. That was before the insanity of a football-focused town had heaped so much condemnation and hurt onto a teenage boy that he'd run away with the rodeo.

"Ralph was my grandpa. She talks to him a lot."

"Did the doctors say anything?" Allison folded a blue fleece throw into a neat square. "About her mental state, I mean?"

"No. I'm worried, though. I wonder if she'll be able to live alone again."

"You're not planning to stay?"

"Not long. Maybe until after Christmas." He jerked one shoulder. "I gotta make a living."

A massive wave of disappointment drenched her good mood. A short stay was better, safer, sensible, but Allison didn't like it.

A stack of nighties in her hand, she pondered her reaction. She was an adult now, not a dewy-eyed teenager in love with the only boy who'd ever kissed her.

Like that made one bit of difference when it came to Jake Hamilton.

Jake saw a range of emotions flicker across Allison's face. Disappointment, worry, relief. He latched on to the last one. She wanted him gone. Out of sight, out of mind. Away from the town that revered Buchanons and loathed Jake Hamilton.

Then why was she here? Why did she insist on pushing past his caution when absolutely nothing good could come of it?

He zipped open a tired blue suitcase, a throwback to the sixties, to find a stack of underwear. Not his favorite thing to unpack with Allison in the room.

His brain had a sudden flashback, a suppressed memory of pink and lace he never should have seen.

He glanced at her. Did she remember, too?

Allison was beside him in a second. "Let me do that."

She grabbed the stack from his hands as he crouched toward the opened drawer. They knocked heads.

"Ow!" Allison sat back on her haunches and laughed. "Hard head."

"I was about to say the same thing." In truth, her head was harder on the inside than on the outside. The woman never gave up, a trait that would leave her disappointed and hurt.

They were a foot apart in front of Granny Pat's oak dresser, on their toes, both holding to a stack of ladies' lingerie, and Jake wished for the thousandth time he could erase one terrible day from their lives. He was comfortable with Allison, *liked* her, a dangerous thing, then and now. She made him smile. She even made him believe in himself. Or she once had. With everything in him he wanted to know this grown-up Allison, a dangerous, troubling proposition.

"You've grown up." Stupid thing to say, but better than yanking her into his arms—an errant, radical thought worthy of a beating from the Buchanon brothers.

She tilted her head, smile quizzical. "Is that a good thing or a bad thing?"

For him? Very bad. But instead of admitting the truth, he tweaked her flyaway hair and pushed to a stand, distancing himself from the cute temptation of Quinn Buchanon's sister. "I'll drag in more of Granny Pat's stuff while you put this away. Okay?"

As if he wasn't already struggling not to touch her, Allison reached out a hand. What could he do except take hold and help her up?

A mistake, of course.

Her skin was a thousand times softer than he remembered and smooth as silk. His rough cowboy hand engulfed her small one. He was nowhere near as tall as her brothers, but he towered above Allison. What man wouldn't understand this protective ferocity that roared in his veins?

Allison had definitely grown up.

And Jake Hamilton was in major trouble.

Chapter Three

Monday morning, Jake drove the dusty graveled road past rows and rows of fence line leading to the Double M Ranch two miles and a world away from Gabriel's Crossing. Multicolored Brahma brood cows grazed peacefully in this section of Manny Morales's pasture land. Not one of them looked up as Jake roared by and pulled beneath the Double M crossbars.

In the near distance, a sprawling ranch house sat like a brick monument to the success of a Mexican immigrant whose work ethic and cattle smarts had created a well-respected bucking bull program. Jake knew. He'd worked for Manny before the Buchanons and the rodeo had given him reason to leave Gabriel's Crossing.

Dust swirled around the truck tires as he parked and got out. Manny, short and stout and leathery, stood in the barn entrance, white Resistol shading his eyes.

"Manny!" Jake broke into a long stride, eager to see his friend and mentor.

"Is that you, Jake boy?" The older man propped a shovel against the barn and came to meet him.

With back slaps and handshakes, they greeted one another. "Manny, it's good to see you."

"Why didn't you tell me you was coming?"

"Why? Would you have cooked for me?"

Manny laughed. He could wrangle a cow, ride a horse

and haul a dozen bulls all around the region, but he couldn't boil water. "Paulina will be crazy happy. She'll want to cook *cabrito* and have a fiesta!"

Jake laughed for the first time since his arrival three days ago in Gabriel's Crossing. "No need to kill the fatted goat. I'll be satisfied with some frijoles and her homemade tortillas."

"Sure. Sure." Manny clapped him on the shoulder again. "But first you got to see your bulls."

"How are they doing?"

Manny's black eyes crinkled at the corners. "You see for yourself. They're good."

Together they made their way inside the enormous silver barn where Manny's dark green Polaris ATV was parked. In minutes, they'd bumped across grassy yellowing fields to a pasture where a dozen bull calves grazed.

"I moved the big boys to the west pasture, closer to the house so I can keep an eye on them," Manny said as he climbed out of the Polaris. "Mountain Man is cranky sometimes so he has his own lot. You saw him buck in San Antonio."

Jake nodded. Chance meetings at rodeos were one of the perks of having a friend in the stock business. "He's a good bull. Some of the cowboys are afraid of him."

"Ah, he's not so bad."

Jake differed in opinion. Mountain Man, a white monster of a bull, was big and bad with the horns to end any discussion. He was also an athlete, hard to ride and keeping his owner in tamales. Manny hauled him to rodeos every week during the season.

"There are your sons," Manny said as he propped a boot on an iron gate and pointed toward the herd.

His sons. Likely the only ones he'd have for a long time. Not that he wouldn't love a family. A stray like him had dreams. A big ranch and plenty of money. Then a woman to love and a few kids. Maybe a lot of kids. If Allison Buchanon intruded on those dreams at times, he'd learned to shut her out and focus on the first part. A ranch. His bulls.

Over the past several years he'd searched out and bought the best young calves he could afford and partnered with Manny to finish and train them.

Their expense, along with the cost of the brood cows, meant a tight budget most of the time but eventually, he'd reap the benefits of his sacrifice. He'd start a ranch of his own and hopefully be able to retire from the circuit. The past couple of seasons had taken a toll on his body and his bank account. At twenty-seven, he was still fit, but a bull rider never knew how long before the constant pounding ended his career. Even now, his shoulder predicted rain before the meteorologists.

"How's the training going?" he asked. "Is Big Country about ready for the circuit?"

Though Jake had borrowed heavily to buy him, Big Country was the animal Jake counted on to make his name in the stock contracting business.

"You'll have to stick around Gabriel's Crossing for a while and find out for yourself, my friend."

"Can't stay long, Manny." He tried to keep the worry from his voice. "But I'm here until Granny Pat is better." Even if it meant dealing with the Buchanons and dwindling cash flow.

"Maybe you stay for good this time. Gabriel's Crossing is your home."

Jake looked out over the cattle—his cattle—and thought of how often he'd longed to go back in time before he'd ruined everything. Before regret and rodeo were his daily companions. Back when he'd been a part of this town and the big Buchanon clan.

"Water under the bridge, Manny. The rodeo can't get along without me." Which wasn't exactly true. Most seasons, he made a living, and arena dust got in a man's blood. But he was sick and tired of the travel and the loneliness.

Manny's dark gaze pierced him. "Still the bad blood?"

No point hiding from Manny. "Buchanons practically own this town. Coming back, even for a while, isn't easy."

Manny sighed and folded his brown, leathery hands on the iron railing. "The Buchanons are good people. By now, they will forgive you. Huh? You talk to them. Find out. Maybe you carry a burden for nothing."

"I don't think so, Manny. I talked to Allison."

"You still sweet for that Buchanon girl?"

Jake felt a lot of things for Allison Buchanon that he couldn't put a name to. Things he couldn't allow into the conversation. Now or ever. "That was a long time ago. Before I ruined everything."

If time healed wounds—and he prayed every night the Buchanons would heal—they didn't need reminders of him to rip open the scab.

He swallowed the taste of regret. He didn't like thinking about the accident, the worst day of his life, but the burden rode his back like a two-ton elephant. He could never forget it. Ever.

The accident *or* the girl.

Buchanon Construction was nothing more than a metal warehouse full of equipment with an office tacked on to one end. Inside that office at a U-shaped desk, Allison entered data for the Willow Creek project into her computer while blonde Jayla fielded phone calls and met with vendors selling ceramic tile or the latest eco-friendly appliances. The place was messy, practical and, other than the desk, bore little resemblance to a business office.

Not that she was thinking about business today with Jake Hamilton lurking in every thought.

Jake. The time at Miss Pat's had been fun and eye-opening. She liked the handsome cowboy as much as ever. His gentle concern for his grandmother tugged at her, but more than that, being with him reminded her of what they'd had, of what might have been.

Jake was unfinished business.

Her twin brothers, Dawson and Sawyer, ambled in from the warehouse, smelling of sweat and doughnuts. "Mirror" twins, her brothers were lady magnets with black hair, blue eyes and bodies honed by years in the hands-on construction business.

Dawson's dimple was on display because both men wore possum grins as if they knew a secret. Allison was relieved to see them smiling this morning. If they'd heard about Jake's return, they wouldn't be smiling.

"You can't hide those from me. I have a nose for fresh-baked anything." Allison held out a hand. "Gimme."

"Greedy, isn't she, Dawson?" Sawyer pulled a doughnut box from behind his back and held the white container above his head. At nearly a foot taller than Allison's five-one, he had a distinct advantage.

"You want me to hop and jump and try to reach them while you laugh at me, don't you?"

"Torment is our game. Hop, little sister."

When she propped a hand on one hip and glared, he wiggled the box and said in a cajoling voice, "Come on. Hop. You know you want a hot, fresh doughnut from The Bakery."

"Well, okay, if I must..." But instead of playing her brother's ornery game, she poked a finger in his relaxed belly. His six-pack abs tightened, and when he curled inward with a "Hey!" Allison laughed and snatched the still-warm doughnut box.

"Greedy *and* sneaky," she said as she popped open the box. "Yum. Maple with coconut. Did you bring milk?"

"Quinn's supposed to be making fresh coffee in the back."

"He's so domestic." She bit into the sweet dough and sighed, her mouth happy with the warm maple goodness.

"Don't let him hear you say that."

"Those things will give you a heart attack." This from Jayla who held a palm over the telephone receiver. "I'm on hold about the Langley license."

None of her three siblings paid Jayla any mind.

"Hey, Quinn," Sawyer yelled toward the back of the warehouse. "What's the holdup on that java?"

Quinn's head appeared around the door leading into the warehouse. Golden haired and pretty, Allison thought he resembled a younger, bigger Brad Pitt.

"Some people work for a living." He gave them all a scowling once over and disappeared again.

"I guess I'll make the coffee." Dawson headed into the warehouse, returning a short time later with a full carafe and a stack of disposable foam cups. "He's in a happy mood today."

"Which means he's not," Jayla said. "The Bartowskis asked for changes to the plans he finished over the weekend. Major changes."

Sawyer snarled. "I hate when that happens."

"He threatened to let Dawg bite them."

"He *is* in a bad mood. Dawg wouldn't bite a hot doughnut. Well, maybe he would, but you get the point." Dawson leaned around the opened doorway. "Hey, Quinn, want a doughnut? Guaranteed to sweeten you up."

A muffled reply about exactly what Dawson could do

with his doughnuts had the siblings stifling snorts that would not be appreciated. They were loud enough, however, that Quinn stalked into the room, hazel eyes shooting sparks. "Something funny?"

Dawg low-crawled from behind Quinn and collapsed at Allison's feet. "You're scaring Brady's dog. Where is Brady anyway?" She tossed the mutt a hunk of sweet roll. He snapped it in midair and tail-thumped in expectation of more.

"Open your mouth, Quinn," she said, "and I'll toss *you* a chunk."

Quinn fisted a hand on his hip and allowed a grudging lip twitch. "You'd miss."

"Can't miss something that big."

"Old joke, sis." But with his better hand, he took a chocolate-covered pastry from the box. "Pour me a cup?"

Dawson obliged, handing the steaming brew to his brother. Quinn shifted the doughnut to his weaker right side to accept the coffee.

"Stinks about the plans." Dawson lifted his ball cap and scratched at his unruly black waves.

"Part of the job." As architect of Buchanon Construction, Quinn developed all their housing concepts, a recent turn of events, considering the slide into depression that had taken him away from home for too long. Even now, he wasn't the most social Buchanon. "Those plans were exactly what they asked for. Now they want changes. I have a feeling this project may not be our favorite."

"We could subcontract the entire project if the Bartowskis become a problem," Dawson said.

"That would only make things worse. If a sub messes up, we're responsible."

"Put Charity on them." Sawyer studied the Bavarian cream inside his doughnut. "This stuff is good."

The oldest of the siblings at thirty-three, Charity was the real estate whiz, slick as a used car salesman, a trait Allison found out of sync with the sweet-faced wife of a deployed navy pilot and the mother of a six- and an eleven-year-old.

"Nah, I'll make the changes. Once." Quinn ripped off a piece of his chocolate doughnut and tossed it to Dawg. Pathetically grateful, dog sat at his feet, begging for more. "Where are we on the Willow Creek project? Any news on the permits?"

Jayla's long hair swayed as she thumped the telephone receiver into its cradle and swung around to face them. "That was Brady. Permits are ready. He's at the court-house now, and says he will meet you two—" she pointed at Sawyer and Dawson "—at the job site. Bring Dawg."

Quinn crossed the small space and kissed the top of her head. "You're amazing." He ripped off another piece of doughnut and held it in front of her nose. "Eat this."

She made a horrified face and squeezed her eyes closed. "Death in a doughnut. I'll pass."

He laughed and popped the bite into his mouth. "Don't know what you're missing, baby sister."

They were hassling Jayla about her rigid eating habits when the front door slammed open, and Brady strode inside.

"Weren't you going to the job site?" Jayla's question fell into the sizzling air and withered away, unanswered.

If a man could spit nails, Allison thought this might be the time to duck and run. With his warrior size, Brady was as dangerous as a rattler when stirred up. And something had definitely stirred him up this morning.

Allison was afraid she knew the cause.

The other siblings exchanged looks. The twins shrugged in unison. No one else had a clue to Brady's fury.

With a dread heavier than a forklift, Allison put her half eaten doughnut on a skinny strip of napkin and waited for the ax to fall.

Voice tight and low, steam all but pumping from his ears, Brady asked, "You haven't heard, have you?"

Quinn set his mug down. "Heard what?"

Blood rushed against Allison's temples. Oh, yeah, here came trouble.

"Jake Hamilton is in town."

Sawyer's jaw hardened. "What?"

"You heard me right. Jake's back."

"Where did you hear that?" Quinn's voice was quiet. Too quiet.

"Courthouse." Brady fisted huge hands on his hips. "I saw the lowlife with my own eyes. Miss Pat's out of the nursing home and Jake's moved in, supposedly to take care of her."

All eyes swung toward Quinn. Like the rest of them—except Allison—he looked stunned. A long beat passed while they absorbed the news. Then, without a word, Quinn spun on his steel-toed boots and left the room.

Chaos erupted.

As if the russet-haired Brady had announced an eminent asteroid collision with downtown Gabriel's Crossing, everyone talked at once. The general consensus was outrage. Outrage that Jake Hamilton would strut into town years after the fact and behave as if nothing had happened. As if he hadn't ruined a man's life.

"Don't you think you're overreacting?" As soon as the words were out, Allison clapped a hand over her mouth. Why had she said that?

Silence descended in a dark, pulsating curtain. Three pairs of eyes aimed at her like hot, blue lasers.

She swallowed. Let reason prevail. *Please Lord.* "Jake's

been gone a long time. His grandma needs him now. We've moved on. Quinn's...okay. We don't even talk about the accident anymore. Can't we let the hard feelings end here and now?"

"You were always on his side." Sawyer's accusation hurt.

"That's not fair. We were all heartbroken for Quinn, even Jake. Quinn was his best friend! He's not some kind of evil monster."

Dawson slapped his cap against his thigh. "Tell that to Quinn."

Sawyer nodded in agreement. "I think the brotherhood needs to pay the hotshot bull rider a little visit."

Brady crouched to pat his dog. The shaggy mutt rolled onto his back, feet in the air. "I'm in."

Allison exhaled a nervous, worried breath. Her doughnut lay like a rock in her belly. "Just because a man you don't like comes to town to care for his grandmother is no reason for the four of you to go ninja grudge match."

Brady rubbed Dawg's belly, his eyes on Allison. "When that one man destroys my brother's future, I'm not likely to ever forget."

That was the problem. She came from a long line of grudge holders. Granddad Buchanon and his brother didn't speak for the last fifteen years of their lives. All because of a dispute over a used tractor. They were supposed to be Christians, but a Buchanon could sustain anger for a very long time.

Allison saw no point in arguing with her brothers. They were as immovable as a concrete slab.

"You should let sleeping dogs lie. That's all I have to say." She turned and headed around the counter to her computer. "We have work to do."

Brady followed her around the desk, Dawg at his side.

His voice had calmed, but his tone held reinforced steel. "We'll handle Jake Hamilton this time, Allison. You stay away from him."

Allison gave him a mutinous glare. She was getting real tired of hearing that.

Chapter Four

The next morning Jake made the rounds in town. First, to the post office to redirect Granny Pat's mail where a friendly postal clerk he remembered slightly inquired about his grandmother. Then to the bank and finally to the grocery store.

Gabriel's Crossing was a lazy stir of business this early, sunlit morning. Townspeople wandered in and out of stores. Doors slammed. Cars and pickups puttered down a five-block main street still paved with the same bumpy red bricks put there eighty-five years ago.

A truck with a Buchanon Construction sign on the door rolled past. Jake watched it, curious and wary, though the morning sun blasted him in the eyes, so he couldn't clearly see the man at the wheel.

Allison had been at the house again last night. Her visits stirred him up and interfered with his sleep. Her and the musty smell of sheets he should have washed before bringing Granny Pat home. A man didn't always think of those things, especially a man who was accustomed to sleeping in his truck or cheap motels along the rodeo circuit.

He both dreaded and longed for evening when Allison would return. She'd promised Granny. Why had she done that? And why couldn't he find the initiative to be somewhere else when she arrived?

Heaviness weighed on his shoulders like a wet saddle

blanket. That's what Gabriel's Crossing did to him. When he was on the road or in his trailer in Stephenville, he seldom dwelled on the tragedy. He'd learned to let it go or go crazy. But here, in Gabriel's Crossing, where memories lingered around every corner and Allison popped in unexpectedly, he thought of little else.

He felt as trapped as a bull in a head gate, unable to go forward, and he sure couldn't go back.

Inside the quiet IGA, Jake pushed a shopping cart down the produce aisle. He wasn't much of a cook but Granny Pat needed nourishing foods to rebuild her strength. A woman who'd cooked from scratch her whole life wouldn't stand for frozen dinners or pizza delivery either. He added a head of lettuce, some tomatoes and a bag of carrots to the cart. Salad. He could do salad. And steak. Big, juicy T-bones with loaded baked potatoes.

He tossed in a bag of potatoes and headed for the meat. The aisles were narrow, a throwback to earlier times, but he'd not been in the mood for the supercenter this morning. Too many people. Too many opportunities to run into someone he didn't want to see.

He wasn't afraid to climb into the chute with an eighteen-hundred-pound bull, but he was a coward in his hometown. The knowledge aggravated him so much Jake considered reshelving the groceries and driving out to the supercenter. If he hadn't promised to meet the home health nurse in an hour, he would have.

As it was, he threw a few more items into the cart and headed for the checkout. A flaming redhead with a snake tattoo down one arm and a dragon from neck to chin rang up the purchases. Gabriel's Crossing had certainly changed. But then, so had he.

The redhead gave him a friendly smile. "Coach Hammonds brought in the football schedules yesterday. Want one?"

She offered a small cardboard card similar to the wallet schedules he remembered.

"I'm good." He would not be attending any football games.

"Oh, well. They're free." She tossed the schedule inside one of the grocery sacks. "You must be new in town. I don't think I've seen you around."

Jake was not about to make a fuss over a high school football schedule even though the red-and-white piece of card stock was a reminder he didn't want.

"Visiting my grandma."

"That's nice." The register beeped as she slid lettuce across the conveyer. "Are you a real cowboy?"

"Nah, I just found the hat." He softened the joke with a smile.

Her hand paused on the T-bone package. She giggled. "You're teasing me, aren't you?"

"Yeah, I am. Sorry. I ride bulls."

Her eyes widened. "No way. That is so scary."

If he lived to be a hundred, he'd always enjoy that kind of reaction, as if he was something special because he wasn't afraid to get on a bull. "Only if I don't stay on."

Which had happened way too often this season.

Another customer pulled into the lane behind Jake. Bolstered by the friendly cashier, he turned to acknowledge the woman, and his heart tumbled.

"Allison."

"Jake, hi." Her wide smile did crazy things to his head. "What are you doing?"

"He's visiting his grandma," Tattoo Girl said as the register beeped and plastic crinkled. "Isn't that sweet?"

Allison's eyes danced with merriment. "He's a sweetie, all right. Are you shopping for Miss Pat?"

"I'm not much of a shopper, but yeah, sort of. I wasn't sure what to buy."

"She made a list. Didn't you bring it?"

Ah, man. The note was sticking on the refrigerator. "Forgot about it."

Allison backed her cart out of the checkout. "I remember. Go ahead and pay out and then we'll go again."

He should refuse, but he couldn't. When it came to Allison Buchanon he didn't have a lick of sense.

Jake glanced at Tattoo Girl who hiked one shoulder and said, "Why not?"

He could think of a lot of reasons.

By the time he paid out and found Allison, an easy task in the small family-run store, she was pondering the brands of laundry soaps.

"I can't remember if she said Tide or Cheer."

Jake studied the detergent as though they mattered. "Pick one. I don't care. I'll be doing the laundry."

"Do you know how?"

"Allison." He grabbed a box and sent it thudding into the basket. "Single guys learn to do laundry or go dirty. I prefer not to smell like the bulls I ride."

"But you don't cook." So small she barely reached his shoulders, she gazed up at him through big brown eyes he'd never forgotten. Did she have any idea how pretty she was?

"How do you know I can't cook?"

"I saw your shopping cart." She made a cute face. "Steaks and salad are a guy's go-to meal. And then you're done."

Jake let a smile creep up his cheeks. "Wise guy." Though she was anything but a guy. Little Allison had grown up. "I don't suppose you'd take pity on a man for eating out a lot."

She tossed in a box of fabric softener sheets and pointed to the west. "Next aisle over. Come on. We'll stock the cabinets."

"Who's going to cook?"

Her answer nearly stopped his heart. "Me."

So much for avoiding Allison Buchanon.

Allison left the warehouse office at five-thirty, stopped at The Bakery to discuss Faith's cake with Cindy, the best and only wedding cake decorator in Gabriel's Crossing, and then headed toward Faith's house.

Jake's truck was noticeably absent as she drove past the Hamilton place, and if she was disappointed, she tried not to be. She'd see him tonight, though she questioned her sanity, as well as her family loyalty. At the same time, she wanted to be there for Miss Pat, a woman who'd taught all the Buchanon kids in first grade. And Allison loved to cook. Buchanon women were noted for their kitchen gifts.

Right. As if Jake had nothing to do with the buzz of energy racing through her system. A buzz that had begun the moment she'd seen him again and hadn't let up.

She passed two little girls pedaling bikes and pulled to the curb outside the faded red brick where Faith had lived alone with her mother since her parents' divorce twenty years ago.

"The topper is in," she said without greeting when her BFF pushed open the smoked glass door. Tall and narrow, Faith was a bleached blonde with a long face and gray eyes who could play the fiddle and clog at the same time, a feat Allison found both charming and hilarious considering her towering height.

"Did you take a picture?"

"Do birds fly?" Allison whipped out her cell and scrolled to the photo. "The next time you're not tutoring after school, you should stop by and check it out. The cake is going to be gorgeous."

"Ooh, I love this." A pair of silver and crystal hearts twined on a silver base engraved with the initials of the bride and groom. "That's exactly what I had in mind."

"Only the best is good enough for my bestie. How did the dress fitting go?"

Faith made a face. "Let's put it this way. Don't tempt me with ice cream or pizza until after the wedding. One more pound and Clare will have to paint the dress on."

"Tell that to Derrick. He's the one who wines and dines you like a princess."

"One of the many reasons I love the guy."

"Derrick is the steadiest, most dependable man in Texas. You'll be a princess forever."

Faith grinned. "From stork to princess. I love it."

Faith's superior height had made her the object of too many jokes through the years. Though Derrick was two inches shorter, he adored his fiancée the way she was.

Every girl wanted a man like that.

Ever present in her thoughts these days, Jake flashed into her mental viewer. He'd been entertainingly inept at the grocery store, and he'd made her laugh over a can of spinach.

"Stop calling yourself a stork. You know how many times I've wished I was tall enough to reach the second shelf in the kitchen cabinet?"

"I can change a lightbulb without a chair."

"Lucky duck."

Faith laughed and hooked an elbow with Allison. "Come on. I have a stack of RSVPs to go through. Let's see who's coming to the biggest party in town."

With the wedding in three weeks, time was running out for all the last-minute details. "I touched base with the band and the caterer this morning, and scheduled the final fitting with all the bridesmaids."

"And?"

"Everything's a go. The caterer even managed some vegan dishes for Jayla and her friends after I sent over some suggestions."

"She's a genius." They settled side by side on a fawn-colored couch. "So are you. How do you find time for all this?"

"The perks of working for family. When the office is slow, I make calls or run errands."

"Saturday for the bridesmaids, right? What time?" Faith chewed the edge of a fingernail.

"Stop that." Allison swatted her friend's hand. "Ten o'clock. Which reminds me, are you going for acrylic nails or natural?"

"Do you actually think I can keep my hands out of my mouth in the weeks preceding the most important day of my life?"

"Not a chance. Acrylic it is. Have you made the appointment? What about your hair?" Allison went down the list she'd checked and rechecked dozens of times. Faith had been known to forget the details. Allison was a detail girl.

A stack of wedding RSVP envelopes—in the same white pearl as the mountain of invitations the two of them, along with Faith's mother, had addressed weeks ago— waited in a box on the coffee table. "Have you opened any of them?"

"I was waiting for you."

"Good. I want to keep a list."

"And you know I'm lousy with lists."

"Part of your charm. You're marrying a statistician. You

don't have to worry about lists anymore." Allison grabbed a stack and a letter opener. "Put acceptances in the white box, rejections in the blue one."

As they sorted the cards, they talked. About how hard it would be to live three hours apart. About the darling house Faith and Derrick had purchased in Oklahoma City. About the honeymoon in Saint Thomas. If Allison felt a twinge of envy mixed in with her absolute delight for her best friend, she didn't acknowledge it.

"Derrick's brother is pretty cute, don't you think?" Faith's voice was casual but she didn't look at Allison, a sign she was trying—and failing—to be subtle.

"Yes, and nice, too, like Derrick."

"And? He's the best man. You're the maid of honor. Maybe you could get something going, and we could be sisters-in-law?"

Allison laughed. "Marrying your husband's brother would not make us related. Besides, I like being single."

"You do not. We've both waited long enough. Now that I'm getting married, you should get serious about finding someone."

She'd found someone once-upon-a-fairy-tale. But her fairy tale had turned into a horror flick.

In self-defense, she said, "I went to the movies with Billy last month."

"Last month! Allison, do you know how pathetic that is? And you only went with him because his sister asked you to take pity on him." Faith put the stack of envelopes in her lap. "Jake's the problem, isn't he? Like always."

Was she that transparent?

"Maybe." Probably. "But that was years ago."

"You still have his picture in your wallet."

"I never got around to taking it out."

"You've changed wallets a dozen times since then.

Which means he's still stuck in your head and your heart. So now that he's back you need to do something about him."

"And cause the biggest war since the Hatfields and McCoys?" Allison shook her head. "I only want to make things easier for him. Our teenage romance is long behind us."

Faith rolled her eyes. "Oh, please. This is me you're talking to. You have never—I repeat *never*—laid to rest the issue of Jake Hamilton. Every guy is measured up against your handsome cowboy, and then you kick them to the curb like a pop can."

Allison sighed. Faith was right. Even when she'd wanted to move on and forget her feelings for Jake, she never had. They'd been prematurely interrupted and she'd never liked unfinished business. It was so untidy. "I don't know what to do. I wish my brothers could get over themselves."

"If wishes were horses. Stop wishing and go for it. Your brothers should have nothing to do with your romantic life, so get to know Jake again and see what happens." Faith ripped open another RSVP. "I have an idea. Invite him to the wedding. We still have invitations."

Allison's heart jumped. "He won't come."

"You never know until you try. Sit right there." Faith pointed at Allison as she hurried out of the room, but stuck her head around the door facing. "Do you want anything to drink while I'm up?"

"Water would be great."

"Got it. I hear Mom in the garage."

While Allison opened, sorted and listed RSVP cards, a nervous pulse ticked in her temple.

The unresolved heartache of a first love that had crashed and burned pushed to the surface like a dead body in water. She had loved him as much as any teenager could. He'd seen her at her worst, her most humiliated, and had never judged her. On the other hand, he'd stood her up at the graduation dance.

Did she really want to revisit either of those places again?

She stared down at the vellum cards and thought of all the weddings she'd attended, of the tiny unacknowledged ache to find her own true love.

Faith was right. She needed to explore this thing with Jake and put the issue to rest once and for all.

"Hello, Allison."

Deep in thought, Allison jumped when Faith's mom, Ellen, trudged into the room wearing blue scrubs, a testament to her nursing job. She wiggled her fingers and padded on silent white shoes down the hall and out of sight.

"Your mom looks tired," she said as Faith returned, bearing a white invitation.

"Eight twelve-hour shifts in a row take a toll."

"Ugh. Poor woman."

"No kidding. I'm glad I went into teaching." With the teacher shortage in Oklahoma, Faith had easily found a new job in Oklahoma City for the spring semester. "I'm filling out this invitation right now, and I want you to hand-deliver it."

Allison returned Faith's grin, though hers was filled with trepidation. "That's easy. I'm going over there when I leave here."

"Cleaning Miss Pat's house is a great excuse to see Jake." Faith pumped her eyebrows.

"Helping an elderly neighbor is not an excuse to see Jake. Stop it!" Allison bit her bottom lip. "I would help Miss Pat even if Jake wasn't there."

"Yes, but you wouldn't enjoy your little trips nearly as much."

True. Painfully true.

She watched Faith write Jake's name in her beautiful script. "Do you think he'll accept?"

Faith slid the card into the envelope and held it out like an Oscar win. "Only one way to find out."

He shouldn't be here. He should get in his pickup and drive out to Manny's.

Jake looked at the spread of vegetables on the kitchen counter and considered sticking everything back in the fridge. Then he could shut off the stove and walk out. Allison would be here any minute.

"Jacob?" Granny Pat's voice wafted in from the living room. "Honey, did you buy cheese for the baked potatoes? Bring me a slice. I haven't had anything but prison food in so long, I'm hungry as a starved wolf."

At the request, Jake resigned himself to letting Allison help him cook dinner. Granny needed this, no matter how hard it was on him.

He took a chunk of cheddar to the recliner where Granny Pat had pretty much lived since coming home. Earlier, the home nurse had gotten her up and walked her to the bath, a trip that had worn her out and torn a strip from Jake's heart.

"Here you go." He went to his knee beside her chair. "Anything else?"

"No, baby." She patted his hand. "You're such a good boy."

The comment made him snort. "Is your memory failing you?"

"I remember everything I want to." She grinned her impertinent grin. "You were always a good boy with a big soft heart. That's why you acted up after your mama left. And you had a right. She broke your little heart in half."

Jake's muscles tightened. He didn't think about his mother much anymore. "I always wondered why she left."

"I know you did, son. Leaving you was wrong of her."

That was the only explanation he'd ever received. His dad was barely cold in the ground before his mother packed her bags and drove away in an old Buick. "Do you ever wonder where she is?"

Granny Pat's winkled face saddened. "All the time, baby boy. For a long time I thought, once she'd grieved your daddy, she'd come back for you."

But she never had. And he'd grown up with a big, gaping hole inside, waiting for his mama to come home and fill it with love.

"I'm not complaining. You took good care of me."

She'd done her best. In between work and her grief over the loss of a son, his grandmother had done all she knew to deal with a sad little boy and later, a wild teenager. Still, he wondered what might have been.

Outside a car door slammed. Jake shook off the uncomfortable nostalgia and jerked to his feet. "Allison's here."

"Ralph thinks you're still sweet on her."

He tried to laugh her off. "You want to get me killed?"

"You've been trying to do that yourself for years."

A man with nothing to lose made a good bull rider.

At the knock, he ignored his grandmother's keen insight to let Allison in. "Hey."

"Hey, yourself." She shoved a bag at him. "Put this in the kitchen while I bring in the casserole."

"Casserole?"

"Mama's chicken spaghetti."

Granny Pat's voice sailed across the room. "I love that stuff."

"I thought we were cooking." Jake looked over one shoulder. "I already put the steaks in the oven."

"For tomorrow," Allison said. "You know how Mom is. She still cooks for an army in case one or two of us kids drops in. She had an extra and I 'borrowed it.'"

Karen Buchanon had fed him for years when he'd tagged along with the four Buchanon boys. Now, he was as grateful as he'd been back then, and the throb of longing was every bit as raw.

He set the bag of what appeared to be cleaning supplies on a table beside the door and followed Allison to the Camaro. Wearing a tan skirt and crisp white shirt with a collar, her flyaway hair bounced as she walked. He liked her hair, itched to touch the silk of it and wanted to kick his own tail for even thinking about her that way.

He had to stop this. Had to stop it now.

His longer stride caught up to her quickly. "Did your mother know you were coming over here?"

"She was going to bring the casserole herself. I volunteered."

"She must not know I'm home."

Allison shrugged. "She wasn't wild about me seeing you, but I make my own choices and she knows that. Besides, she and Miss Pat go way back." She handed him the still-warm container. "Mom takes care of her friends."

Right. Karen Buchanon would visit Granny Pat even if her grandson was Ted Bundy.

"Neither of you mentioned this little errand of mercy to your brothers, did you?"

"You're cranky today."

"Did you?"

"No. They might do something stupid. They've been threatening—" She stopped halfway to the house and slapped her hands on her hips. "I want this to stop. You got me to admit my brothers still hold a grudge, and I didn't want to go there. Does that make you happy?"

With her face tilted toward his and her brown eyes snapping, she was cute as a kitten. Adorable and off-limits.

"Happy? Hardly." But exactly what he'd expected. Not what he'd hoped for or even dreamed of, but exactly what he deserved.

She hadn't intended to discuss her brothers. He could see that and understood. Now, she was furious, both at herself and him, for opening up the sore topic.

Unlike Brady Buchanon whose temper was renown, Allison's fury wouldn't last long. She was too good, too generous, too kind. And she was tearing him apart.

Resigned to spend the evening fighting memories, he led the way into the kitchen where the smell of broiling steak overpowered the small space.

"Better check this," he said and peaked inside the oven. "Looking good."

So was Allison.

He watched her move to the outdated sink and glance out the window toward the darkened backyard.

"Remember that time we grilled steaks for Dad's birthday and the dog ate yours?"

He smiled at the memory. At the woman. "You gave me half of yours."

"I could never eat a whole one anyway." She gazed around the room. "Where's the steak sauce and all the fixings we bought?"

He wished she wouldn't say *we.* It sounded way too cozy. "In the fridge."

"Okay." Allison went to the refrigerator and pulled out sour cream, cheese, butter, steak sauce and bacon bits and set them on the small round kitchen table where he and Granny Pat ate their meals. The wooden top was scarred from the number of times he'd done school projects in this kitchen with Granny Pat's assistance. He never wanted to minimize what his grandmother had done for him. She'd been there when his mother had refused to be.

What was wrong with a kid that his own mother could walk out and never call, never even send a birthday card? For years, on his birthdays, he'd thought for sure she would remember him. She never had.

Memories were thick as swamp mosquitoes tonight.

To break his runaway thought train, Jake opened the overhead cabinet and eyed the questionably clean plates. "Should I rinse these off?"

"Have they been washed since you've been here?"

"First home-cooked meal."

"Better rinse." As he reached for three white plates, she moved from the table to his side. "I have something for you."

He set the plates in the sink with a clatter. "For me?"

Allison held a white envelope toward him.

Puzzled, he accepted the fancy envelope. As he did, Jake examined the rise of pleasure, the unspoken need to reconnect with things better left alone. Hadn't he just been thinking about a birthday card, though his birthday was long past? "What is this?"

"Open the envelope and see for yourself."

Curious, Jake removed a pretty scripted invitation and read. His belly dropped to his boots. "Are you serious? Faith is inviting me to her wedding?"

"Don't say no, Jake. Please come."

He shook his head, though his chest expanded with want and hope. "You're crazy."

"And your steaks are burning."

He whipped around to remove the meat, clattering the pan onto the stove top. Sizzle and fragrant smoke filled the air.

With a growl, he said, "I told you I couldn't cook."

"Which is why I'm here. Put the steaks in the warmer. I'll make salad and rinse the plates. You get Miss Pat ready to pig out. We're going to fatten her up."

There she went again, using the *we* word. He closed his eyes and gave his head a little shake. If Allison insisted on coming around on a regular basis, something was bound to explode. Either him or her brothers, and neither was a pretty thought.

He shoved the white envelope into his back pocket.

Inviting him to a wedding with all the Buchanons and half of Gabriel's Crossing? Was she insane? Did she want to ruin her friend's big day?

This new adult Allison was even more of a Pollyanna eager to fix the world than she'd been as a teen.

And she was killing him. Absolutely killing him.

Chapter Five

Jake's tenderness with his grandmother brought a lump to Allison's throat just as being here caused a twinge of disloyalty. Mom hadn't been pleased, though she'd relented for the sake of Miss Pat. Still, Allison couldn't help feeling guilty. Was Faith correct? Was Allison using Miss Pat as an excuse to see Jake?

The three of them sat at the scarred table with Miss Pat on a pillow to cushion her bony body against the hard surface. Jake had carried her to the chair with her hair freshly brushed and wearing a silky Dresden-blue bed jacket. She reminded Allison of a tiny snow-capped bluebird.

"Your robe is beautiful, Miss Pat."

"Jacob bought it when I first went to the hospital. I had to have something decent. Imagine a wrinkled old lady like me wearing one of those silly gowns with the naked behind." She made a face. "Better yet, don't imagine it."

Allison's mouth trembled with a smile. "He has good taste."

"That's what Ralph said. I have a feeling he was a dab jealous of his own grandson. Ralph never bought me anything this fancy. But then, he was a skinflint." She whipped her napkin into her lap. "Yes, you were, Ralph. You know I'm telling the truth."

The conversation with Ralph brought a momentary lull as Jake and Allison exchanged glances.

"Well, Jacob. Are you going to pray or sit there and make goo-goo eyes at Allison?"

Goo-goo eyes? Oh, for crying out loud. Jake spent most of his time glaring at her and trying to run her off. Couldn't Miss Pat see that?

A dull blush darkened Jake's face. He rolled his eyes, but didn't respond to his grandmother's outrageous comment.

"Do you mind if I say grace?" he asked, his camo-green gaze holding hers steady.

"Really?" Jake Hamilton wanted to pray?

His sculpted lips softened into a smile as he shared the good news that he'd become a Christian. Allison's heart jitterbugged with the energy of a 1950s teenager. No wonder he seemed different.

"Changed everything," he said.

"I'm glad, Jake. Thrilled." Beyond delighted.

For Allison, faith had always been a given. She'd grown up in church, and though there were times she struggled to understand why bad things happened, she believed with all her heart in the goodness and power of Jesus. But Jake hadn't been raised to believe. The fact that he'd converted, and that his grandmother had noticed, was huge. As he said, it changed everything.

The one fly in her romantic fantasies about Jake had been his lack of faith.

Oh, my. This was wonderful and scary and promising. And she was out of her mind.

Allison dropped her head and squeezed her eyes shut as Jake's low rumble asked the blessing on the meal.

Please, she prayed. *Let this make a difference to my brothers.*

She prayed this would change things between Jake and her family. The Buchanons had taken Jake to church on occasion, but he'd never embraced their faith. Until now. Surely, the brothers would forgive him now. Wouldn't they?

All through the meal, hope rode Allison's shoulders like a winged creature. Buoyed by the good news, she teased conversation out of Jake and relished Miss Pat's feistiness. The meal lingered for much longer than required to eat the simple food. Dishes were pushed aside and elbows propped on the table as they caught up on the years apart.

Something inside Allison centered. She'd missed their friendship, their talks and hanging out. She may have crushed on Jake as a teenager, but he'd been her buddy, too.

"You're tired, Granny Pat," Jake said when the older lady began to nod.

Miss Pat's head snapped up. "I know it. Silly old body of mine." She pointed a bony finger toward the cheese. "Cut me a slab of that, will you, honey? It's from IGA."

"You mentioned that earlier, Granny Pat," Jake said gently.

"I told *you,* not Allison. Stop acting like I've lost my mind. It makes me and Ralph both mad enough to spit."

Allison caught Jake's eye as she sliced the cheese. Miss Pat's body might be weak but there was nothing weak about her spirit.

"With your spunk, Miss Pat, you'll be back on your feet before Christmas."

"You got that right, honey." She waved the cheese at Jake. "Take me and my cheese to my room. I'm done in."

"Yes, ma'am. At your service." He scraped back his chair and tenderly lifted his grandmother. "You sure smell pretty."

"You sure tell tall tales." She patted his cheek. "Love you, Jacob."

He kissed her cheek. And Allison melted like chocolate on s'mores.

To get herself under control, she leaped up and began clearing the table. She hadn't intended to linger like a lovesick kid. Faith was to blame—Faith and her matchmaking ideas and her wedding invitation.

She glanced at the clock, saw the time was already growing late. She hadn't even begun cleaning the house, a promise she intended to keep.

Not that she minded another trip or two. As long as her brothers didn't know.

She scraped the dishes and put them into the dishwasher, thinking about the grown-up Jacob. In the years in between, he'd developed a cowboy swagger. He also hid his feelings better than he had as a boy, so that she was not quite sure where they stood. Not like before when she'd read him as easily as a Pre-Primer. The adult Jake was more controlled, too, not the wild, impulsive kid who'd vandalized a Buchanon construction site after the accident that had left Quinn with a crippled arm. And if his care for Miss Pat was any indication, he was even more tenderhearted, a trait he covered with attitude and silence. Beneath his rodeo-tough exterior, he'd always been a marshmallow, though her family didn't see him through her eyes.

From their dinner conversation, she'd learned about his rodeo career and the bulls he kept at Manny Morales's ranch. She'd also learned from a slip by Miss Pat of the Wyoming woman he'd almost married. Her heart had stopped beating on that one, though Jake had laughed off the reference and refused to discuss it.

"You should go on home."

She glanced over her shoulder to see the handsome cowboy enter the kitchen. He looked good in the faded-blue chambray shirt and old jeans, his dark hair trimmed and neat, his shoulders and arms muscled by hours of training. A lean teenager had gone away. A heartbreaker had returned in his place.

"I haven't cleaned yet."

"I'll take care of it."

"Don't push me out, Jake. You know I won't go back on my promise to Miss Pat."

"She'll understand."

"I wouldn't."

He came across the room and took the salad bowl from her hand, his voice low. "Why are you playing with fire when you know we'll both get burned?"

"Rebellion is in my blood." She gave him a perky grin and stuck the meat tray in the sink.

"Your brothers wouldn't like it if they knew you were here."

"Since when have my brothers run my life? You know me better than that. They didn't then, and they don't now. Especially now."

"I don't want to stir up trouble, Allison."

"Are you calling me trouble?" She took a step closer, challenging.

His nostrils flared. "What do you think?"

"I think we can be friends again. Like before."

His gaze dropped to her mouth. The air between them shivered with possibility.

Did the tough bull rider remember that night? That first and last kiss?

"I don't want to hurt anyone," he murmured.

The truth in his statement was a stark reminder that people had been hurt, including the two of them. "I don't either. That's the whole point, Jake," she said softly. "Hurt never goes away unless we choose to release it."

He was standing really close, and she could smell the faint scent of aftershave and steak sauce, a funny combination but pleasantly male. She wanted to walk right into his arms and see if they fit together the way she remembered. Though he'd only kissed her once, she'd never forgotten, and now she understood why. Faith was right. Every boy had been compared to that one defining moment. Compared and rejected. Jake had always been the one.

Oh, my. Life had suddenly become much more complicated.

"I wish letting go was that easy," he murmured, near enough that she read the wistfulness in his green eyes.

"Come to Faith's wedding." Suddenly, she wanted him there with all her heart. Somehow, together, they'd find a way to make things right again.

His laugh was a short bark. "Yeah, like that's going to fix everything."

"Being there might be a start." She touched his arm. "Please. I want you to come. You have a right to be there."

He pressed his lips into a thin line and looked beyond her toward the window above the sink. When his gaze returned to hers, the green eyes held a look she didn't understand, but he said, "Let me think about it."

That was as good as she was going to get, and Allison decided to take hope and run. Let him fret over the invitation. Let him wonder what it would be like to be back among friends who'd helped shape his childhood. Let him yearn for something more, in the same way she had yearned for him, though until this moment, she'd not acknowledged that longing.

"Think about the invitation all you want as long as you show up at Faith's wedding with your dancing shoes on. Now, grab the Windex and a rag. These dirty windows are killing me."

He shook his head. "You're an impossible optimist."

"Yeah, but you like me," she said with a cheeky grin.

He tugged a strand of her hair. "Got me there."

And that little admission fueled her determination to make things right between Jake Hamilton and the Buchanon clan.

Several days later, Jake thought the freezer was well stocked with casseroles, the laundry was caught up and the killer windows gleamed. But Allison showed up at six-thirty anyway. As always, he made a halfhearted attempt to send her home but she called him grumpy and sailed right inside.

He had to admit her company was a welcome break from worrying over bills and his grandmother. And yeah, he looked forward to the moment each evening when a little bundle of sunshine lit up his day. As long as the Buchanon brothers didn't give her grief, he could deal with the other issues. He didn't want her hurt again, and whether she admitted it or not, she had been. He'd done enough damage in this town.

"What did you do today?" she asked, frowning around the somewhat cluttered room. He'd picked up his socks and put away the dishes. Wasn't that enough?

"Besides aggravating my grandmother until she ran me off?" He cast a look toward the chair where Granny napped. "I took a drive out to Manny's while the nurse was here."

"How are they?" Allison tossed a tiny shoulder bag onto the couch and made herself at home. "I haven't seen them in town in a while."

"They're good." He patted his pocket for his cell phone. "I need to give Paulina a call. She invited us out for dinner, but Granny isn't up for the travel."

"I will be soon." Jake and Allison turned toward Granny Pat whose sharp gaze rested on them. "Why don't you two kids run on out there without me."

Jake shook his head even though his heart had done a weird stutter step. Exactly the way it did each time he eased down on the back of a bull. "What about the casserole I set out of the freezer?"

"I'll eat it. You won't have to worry about feeding me." She shooed him with a skinny, pale hand. "Go on now."

"I don't think that's a good idea."

"This is my house and I want you out for a while. All this moping around gets on my last nerve."

Allison snorted. Jake shot her a scowl. "What are you laughing at?"

"You. Come on, cowboy, before she throws her Sudoku book at you. I want to see your bulls, and pig out on Paulina's enchiladas."

"Who's going to heat her dinner?" As much as he liked the idea of getting out of town, he was careful not to leave Granny Pat alone. And hanging out with Allison was like a death wish. A really pleasant one.

"Flo can use a microwave. Not much else, but she's a whiz of a nuker, and she's on her way."

"I thought she was in Florida on the beach."

Florence Dubois, which he was certain was a stage name, was Granny Pat's longtime friend, a former Las Vegas showgirl with legs like stilts, big hair, and abundant cosmetic surgery.

"*Was.* When she learned I'd finally escaped from prison, she fired up the Winnebago and headed back to Gabriel's Crossing."

"Carson Convalescence is not a prison." He'd made that statement so often, it had become as automatic as blinking.

She flapped her white speckled hand again. "Whatever

you want to call my confinement, I've escaped, and Flo is coming over, and you're going to leave us alone for a while. Get moving."

"Well." He stacked his fists on his hips.

Granny Pat chuckled. "No excuses, Jacob. Go. Enjoy. Paulina cooked and a woman doesn't like to be stood up."

Jake turned to Allison. "What are you grinning about?"

She laughed aloud. "Grab your hat. You've been tossed out."

"Not the first time," he muttered.

The woman didn't realize what she was doing, or if she did, she didn't care.

"My car or your truck?" Allison asked.

"You gonna let me drive your Camaro?"

She snorted. "How about if I drive your big old truck instead?"

"Nobody drives my truck." But he grabbed his hat and followed her out the door.

The ride to the Double M Ranch was bumpy, short and quick. With country music as background and safely out of Buchanon radar range, he let down his guard and listened to Allison rattle about Faith's wedding plans, the big building project out in Willow Creek, a place he didn't even remember, and a hodgepodge of other topics. She jumped from one thing to another like a fluffy little bunny. That's what she reminded him of. Cute and full of energy and soft. He slammed the gate on the last thought. Allison and her softness were off-limits. She was way more than cute. Beautiful. Kind. Warm as a Texas summer.

They could be on friendly terms, as long as her brothers didn't get involved, but he wasn't about to think beyond friendship. As soon as Granny Pat was settled, he was out of here. Let sleeping dogs lie, and escape as soon as possible.

If he didn't get back to work soon, his bank account would suffer and he'd risk falling behind on his loans. Loans that pointed to his future instead of the mess in Gabriel's Crossing and a persistent past that intruded like flies at a picnic.

Occasionally, one of the other Buchanons seeped into the conversation. They'd been as close as family, and sometimes he yearned to be among them so much his chest ached. Being back in Gabriel's Crossing messed with his mind worse than a head slam to the dirt.

"Mom's already packing Christmas packages for all the soldiers in Trevor's unit." Allison sat at an angle in the bucket seat, the console open between them. He was glad for the divider, or he might have done something stupid like reach for her hand.

"Trevor?" he asked, instead.

"Charity's husband. He's with the navy in Africa."

Ah, now he remembered. "She married Trevor Sandifer, right? Didn't they have a kid?"

"Two." She opened the tiny purse and extracted a cell phone. "Want to see their pictures?"

Before he could reply, she stuck the screen in front of his face. He glanced down at a blond boy with blue eyes and then back at the country road. Gravel spewed out behind them, leaving a dust trail.

"That's Ryan. He's eleven."

"He looks like Charity."

"I think so, too. He's a mess sometimes without his daddy here, but a cute mess. Charity has her hands full." She ran her index finger over the screen and produced another photo. "Amber is the dimpled princess of the Buchanon clan. She's in first grade and learning to read. You should hear her. Last night she read to her daddy on Skype, and he got choked up."

"Man. That must be tough."

"Yeah." She put the phone back in her tiny, overstuffed bag. "But they're strong. Trevor will be home in another six months."

"That's good." He'd considered joining the military after the accident. If not for the rodeo he would have. Anything to escape the daily censure, though he had to admit, the inner condemnation had followed him for years.

Another pickup rumbled past in a wake of dust. He wanted to see photos of the other Buchanons, especially Quinn, but wasn't sure he was ready to face what he'd done, even in a picture. "Still have the big Buchanon get-togethers on Sunday?"

"Like always. You should—"

"Don't finish that thought." But the yearning hit him full force. He should come over, like before. While the smell of Mrs. B.'s pot roast or fried chicken filled the house, he could pile up on the floor with the guys and talk football and girls, cars and camo.

He gripped the steering wheel and strained toward the crossbars of Manny's ranch.

Camo. *God, don't let me think about hunting. Don't let my mind go there.*

But the pictures came anyway, flashing through his head like something out of a horror movie.

"Hey." Allison's voice broke through the ugly thoughts. "Earth to Jake."

"Sorry." He was sweating. He cranked up the AC. "There's the ranch."

"Will you let me ride one of your bulls?"

He offered a look meant to quell. "Not in this lifetime."

She snickered. "I was kidding."

"No, you weren't, you little hot dog. But I'll hop on one and impress you with my finesse."

"Remember when you took me to the rodeo in Sand Creek? I was scared to death you were going to get killed."

"That was one of the first times I placed in the short go."

"We had a great day."

"Until Brady found out and you got grounded."

"I wasn't grounded because of you, Jake. I was grounded because I didn't ask permission. I don't have to ask anymore. If I want to go somewhere, I go. We should do it again. When is your next rodeo?"

"You're kind of pushy, aren't you? What if I'm taking someone else?"

"Are you?"

"Maybe." He wasn't, but she was walking on dangerous ground.

His hedge bought him some time. She fell silent, and the turmoil that was Allison Buchanon stirred in his belly. He had no right to be attracted to her, any more than she should be attracted to him. He gnawed the inside of his cheek.

He wasn't attracted. He couldn't be. He'd put all that to rest the day he'd left Gabriel's Crossing for good.

"Hey." Her small hand touched the forearm of his shirt. He could feel her warmth seeping through, the warmth of a relentless optimist with the biggest heart in Texas.

"What?"

"Just hey. I'm glad you're here. I'm glad I'm here."

Oh, boy. "Granny's getting stronger every day. I have to get back pretty soon."

"I know. I know. You're only home through the holidays." She beamed a wide smile that did weird things to his head. "But we can enjoy today."

The truck rumbled to a dust-stirring stop in Manny's driveway. Jake shifted out of gear and with an arm looped over the steering wheel turned toward her. He didn't even want to think about how fresh and pretty she was.

"Ycah," he said, resigned. "I guess we can."

Chapter Six

Jake needed to be alone. He needed to pray. About Allison. About money. About his grandmother.

And so he drove to the Double M where he spent a little time with Manny and Paulina before taking the Polaris out to the bull pasture.

Beneath a leaden sky, a north wind coaxed leaves from trees and hinted at the coming winter, a normally toothless beast in warm-blooded Texoma. Still, something about the autumn pastures and tree-lined creeks brought Jake closer to God. He supposed he and the Almighty had a strange relationship.

He parked the ATV at the pond and, hands deep in his jean jacket, walked around the edge noting deer tracks in the damp red earth. Deer season was upon them. He'd not hunted since the accident. Probably never would again, though he enjoyed a good deer chili.

He squatted on a rock and thought about his job. He was floundering here, growing poorer with each sunrise.

But what was a man to do?

Last night with Allison at the Morales dinner table had been both wonderful and unnerving. He liked her more than he wanted to, more than he should, but every minute spent with her was pure pleasure.

He was one messed-up hombre.

Leaving the Polaris on the pond dam, he walked across

the fields, praying and thinking, though no flaming banner from Heaven answered his queries.

Around him, the woods and fields smelled of damp fallen leaves. Thanksgiving was around the corner and then Christmas. Already, the town workers erected candy cane and snowflake lights along First Street, a jump start on the holiday season.

For once in many years, he wanted to be here for the holidays. Granny wasn't getting any younger, a fact that had slapped him in the face during her months in Carson Convalescence. He regretted the years of phone calls instead of visits, but then he regretted so many failures.

But more than Granny, he wanted to spend Christmas with Allison. He closed his eyes, fought the feelings that swam in on a current of warm pleasure. Allison was a ticking time bomb.

Between now and Christmas stretched a thousand miles of rodeos, and he prayed to make some of those events. A bull rider didn't draw a paycheck unless he rode, and Jake wasn't sure what to do about it. He couldn't leave, wasn't sure he wanted to, but being here cost him.

"In more ways than one, Lord," he said, looking up into a sky scattered with flat gray clouds. The money was one thing. The cost to his heart and soul was another.

He crossed a skinny trickle of water, a natural spring that fed the pond and led to the cross-fenced bull pasture.

The sound of bawling calves reached his ears. He gazed into the horizon to where a young yellow bull bucked and jumped, his strong legs kicking out behind, a champion in the making. All Jake had to do was hold on a little longer and the bulls would make his living for him.

Then he saw something that jammed his breath in his throat. He stopped, squinted, hoping he was wrong. He wasn't.

Two boys ran around inside the gathering pen with a half-dozen young bulls. His bulls. Horned and dangerous.

Jake broke into a lope. "Hey, you boys, get out of there!"

Two heads jerked toward him, one blond and one dark. The blond looked uncannily like the photo Allison had shown him of her nephew.

The boys spotted him and bolted for the gate.

"Hold up!" Jake yelled, but the pair scrambled over the closed gate and ran like rabbits across the pasture in the other direction.

By the time Jake arrived, they had disappeared over the rise. He stood breathless, wondering if he should get the Polaris and give chase but decided against it. They'd be long gone before he could return.

He stared across the fading green pasture toward the gentle slope of land. The boys had disappeared from sight.

When he was their age, he would have pulled the same kind of dangerous stunt. Probably had.

But danger was the point. Messing with bucking bulls, even young ones, could be deadly. They all had horns and even snubbed ones were dangerous. They were all unpredictable. Even grown men with professional training were sometimes badly injured. A boy didn't stand a chance.

He wondered if one of the boys was Allison's nephew, Ryan, but he couldn't be certain. He'd seen only a photo of the kid.

The situation worried him, but he didn't know what to do. Without a positive identification, there were no parents to contact.

After checking his animals to be sure they were all right, he started back to the Polaris.

He'd better warn Manny.

Jake never saw it coming.

He was pushing a borrowed mulcher around the Hamilton yard filled with oak leaves when an unfamiliar Dodge

Ram rumbled to a stop out front. Late model. Shiny red. Nice truck.

Though the autumn temperature was a pleasant fifty, sweat leaked from his body and dripped into his eyes. His damp shirt stuck to him like salty skin. He removed his hat, swiped at the sweat with a blue bandana and watched the doors of the Ram swing open. All four of them.

Everything in Jake went still. The roar in his temples was louder than the mulching engine. He felt dizzy. Sick. And the cause wasn't the sweaty job.

Four Buchanon brothers slid out of the truck and strode toward him across the lawn.

A wild mix of love and sorrow engulfed him.

From the stiff set of their shoulders, this was not a friendly visit. Not that he'd expected one.

Jake killed the machine and waited. Bits of dead leaves and dry grass fluttered to the ground in the sudden silence.

Stride for stride they came like something out of a TV commercial. Not a one of the oversize men wore a welcoming expression.

He was tired and thirsty and about to have to fight four men at once. The old Jake would have lowered his head and, like a mad bull, gone on the attack. His motto had been: "he might go down but he'd get in a few good punches before he did." The new Jake understood. Whatever they chose to do, he had it coming.

Lord, I could use a little wisdom about now.

"Hamilton." Brady Buchanon was six feet six inches of muscles, a warrior on the football field and off, with a temper that had gotten him into a few scrapes over the years.

"Brady." Jake wanted to offer a handshake but knew he'd be rejected. Heck, he wanted to throw his arms around each of them in a man hug. But wanting and reality were as far apart as the earth and moon.

His eyes moved from one brother to the other. His friends. His enemies. How he'd missed them. "Dawson, Sawyer. Quinn."

The blue eyed, black-haired twins stood like bookends with Brady and Quinn in the center.

Jake's gaze centered on Quinn.

His former best friend was still built like an anvil with wide pro quarterback shoulders and a skinny waist. Standing before him was a champion athlete, the golden boy of Gabriel's Crossing, left fist clenched while the right arm curved at his side, smaller than the other. Allison said he was an architect now, but the lost dream hovered in the grass-scented air between them. Jake Hamilton had destroyed Quinn Buchanon's arm and with it his dream.

If he could only go back…

"Nice to see you guys." What else was he supposed to say? He *was* glad to see them. He hurt with the pleasure.

Brady's nostrils flared. Though a good guy who'd give the shirt off his back to a friend, Brady Buchanon was a formidable enemy. They all were. Buchanons protected their own. "This isn't a social call."

"I didn't figure it was." Jake wiped his hands on the bandana and shoved the blue cloth in his back jeans pocket. His throat was dry as sand and he'd give a dollar for a drink of water. "So, why are you here?"

"To offer a warning. Stay away from our sister."

Jake heaved a weary sigh. He'd known Brady would say that. Though he'd managed to keep his friendship with Allison below Buchanon radar for a week, he'd also known this meeting was inevitable. "Have you discussed this with Allison?"

"What are you? A coward hiding behind a girl?" Quinn's lips sneered.

Quinn, his best friend. How many times had he wished

the accident had happened to him instead of this man he'd loved like a brother?

"She's not a little girl anymore, in case you haven't noticed."

"Yeah, well, we don't want you noticing. That's the deal. Stay away from our sister. Stay away from *us*."

Sentiment only went so far. They were starting to get his back up. "I can't stop Allison from visiting my grand-mother."

"We can."

Jake gave a short bark of laughter, incredulous. "Good luck with that."

Brady stepped closer, his massive size intimidating. Jake braced himself to fight or take a beating. "One warn-ing, Hamilton. Back off."

"I'm not here to cause a problem, Brady. I'm here for my grandmother. I can't tell Allison what to do even if I wanted to. Believe me, I've tried. And neither can you."

"She was seen in your truck last night."

So that was the problem. The trip to the ranch for en-chiladas. He wondered what they'd say when they found out—and they would—that Allison spent nearly every evening at the Hamilton house?

"I'll repeat. She's a grown woman, a fact she's made very clear to me."

Sawyer bowed up. "What does that mean?"

Jake shot the twin a narrow look. "You figure it out. Now, if that's all the good news you Buchanons have to share, I have work to finish."

He started to turn away but Quinn stepped forward and grabbed his arm. "We'll say when this conversation is over."

Jake shook him off. "Back off, Quinn."

"Or what, Jake? What are you going to do? Shoot me?"

As if the other man had sucker punched him, the wind went out of Jake. His shoulders slumped. He closed his eyes. In a voice ripped with pain, he said, "Do you know how many times I've wished I could change that day? It was an accident, Quinn. An accident."

"Yeah. What about the illegal booze you *accidentally* brought along?"

The truth was a chain saw tearing through him. Never mind that Quinn had drunk the beer, too. Jake had the fake ID. Jake had bought alcohol on the hunting trip. In the misty morning, with a beer in his brain, he was the one who'd thought he'd seen a deer. *He,* and he alone, had been the one who'd pulled the trigger.

The memory of the report that blasted through the chilly autumn stillness, the thundering exhilaration when what he'd thought was a deer crashed into the brush. But it was Quinn's hoarse scream that haunted Jake, the electric realization that he'd shot his best friend with a deer rifle, a gun powerful enough to destroy bone and nerves and muscles.

He squeezed his eyes shut against the flashing video. Bloodstained grass. The weight of Quinn's much larger body as he'd carried him to the truck. The river of tears he'd wept.

"I was a stupid kid."

"So, don't be a stupid man. Leave the Buchanons alone, and we'll leave you alone." Brady tapped Jake's chest with his index finger. "Got it?"

Jake backed up a step, trying to hold his temper in check. Turn the other cheek. Walk away.

Dawson grabbed his brother's arm. "Come on, Brady. We've delivered the message. Let's go."

"Dawson's right," Sawyer said. "We've got work to do."

Brady stood like a towering giant, stretched to his full height. Intimidating seemed a mild word. Of all the Buchanon men, he was the biggest, and the rest were six footers or better.

With his eyes holding Jake's, Brady said, "You boys load up. I'll be there in a second."

Jake breathed a sigh of relief. One Buchanon alone, he could survive, even if that particular Buchanon was eight inches taller and seventy pounds heavier.

Dawson, ever the sane voice, shook his head. "Not happening. Let's go. We're done here."

"He's right, Brady," Sawyer said, though none of them moved. "Message delivered, and I got a hot date tonight. If we don't finish the framing at the McGowen house, I'll be late."

Brady continued to hold Jake's eyes in a silent challenge, an old game of who would look away first. Jake didn't want to play. He backed down, looked to the side.

Turn the other cheek. Do the right thing.

A brown car puttered to the stop sign. The driver rubbernecked at the men in the yard.

As if satisfied, Brady spun away and walked with his brothers to the truck. Jake stood in the yard, sweating and sad, watching them leave.

Long ago, he would have leaped into the bed of the truck, whooped and pounded the heel of his hand on the cab top and gone with them. It didn't matter where. Anywhere with the Buchanon boys was a good time.

He watched Quinn and saw that the damaged arm was useful as Quinn reached for the truck door. Though weaker and smaller, the arm had function. *Thank you, Lord, for that.*

Throat thick, Jake desperately wanted to make amends. He'd forgotten exactly how desperately until faced with the man whose life he'd ruined.

"Quinn," Jake called, startled to hear his voice but certain he had to say something more, something that mattered.

Quinn turned his head, his injured hand braced against the open door. He didn't speak, only stared at Jake.

The other three Buchanons looked his way. Sun glinted off the truck, gilded them, especially Quinn, the golden boy.

A tumble of emotion rose in Jake's throat, words trapped inside that had no names.

"I—" What did he say? What *could* he say? He'd give his right arm in place of Quinn's? He wished he'd been the victim that November morning?

But he'd said all those things and dozens more, and not a one of them changed anything.

Tension stretched like a wire between Jake and the man he'd wronged. Stretched until it snapped, and the moment passed. Quinn slid into the truck and slammed the door, and the Buchanons drove away.

Allison's first indication that something had gone wrong occurred the moment she entered the office warehouse at nine o'clock Tuesday morning. All five Buchanon men stood in a huddle, voices raised as they talked in strained tones. Even the usually chipper Dawson wore a grim expression. Allison set a steaming caramel latte on the counter, tossed her keys and bag toward her computer and joined them.

She had a jittery feeling that this had something to do with Jake, though it very well might not. Lately, she thought everything related to Jake. Maybe because she couldn't get him out of her head.

"What's going on?" she asked. "Has something happened?"

"Trouble on the McGowen house." This from her

Dad. At sixty-one, he still worked a full day, sometimes more and could build a house from the ground up single-handedly. At times, he was a hard man, and trouble on a job site infuriated him.

Allison's anxiety level decreased. Trouble on the job happened. It had nothing to do with Jake.

"What kind of trouble? Can we get Charity to take care of it?" Vendors and subcontractors sometimes caused delays. Materials were late or subs got tied up on other jobs and put the schedule behind.

"Someone vandalized the property. Spray paint everywhere. Kicked in some walls the boys put up yesterday," her dad said. Never mind that her brothers were grown men who towered over their father. To Dan Buchanon, his sons would always be "the boys." "Made a mess of everything."

"How bad?"

Brady growled like a dog. Dawg, who'd flopped at his master's feet, raised his head. Sawyer tossed him a chunk of muffin, which was deftly caught and swallowed in one motion. "Bad enough to put us behind for a week."

Allison grimaced. Like Dad, Brady ran a tight schedule, balancing more than one project at a time for optimal use of personnel. When the painters were in one house, the plumbers could be in another and the carpenters in yet another. At the moment, he juggled five different projects. A setback anywhere could disrupt the flow of work and seriously annoy her big brother.

Sawyer removed his cap and studied the Dallas Cowboys insignia. "We haven't had vandalism on a site in a long time."

"Years," Quinn said.

"I'm gonna knock some heads over this."

Her dad clapped a hand on Brady's shoulder. "You have to find them first."

"Oh, I'll find them. In fact, I think I know exactly where he is."

A warning buzz tingled up the back of Allison's neck. "You think you know who did this?"

"Yeah."

"Are you thinking who I'm thinking?" Quinn asked.

"I find it too much of a coincidence that Jake Hamilton is back in town and shortly after our unfriendly little talk, we have a project vandalized for the first time in years."

"What unfriendly talk?" Allison asked. "What did you guys do?"

Brady ignored the question. "He did before."

"Answer my question."

"Leopards don't change their spots." Sawyer slapped his cap on. "Maybe we should take another trip to see rodeo boy and see what he has to say for himself."

Allison's pulse jumped. "Another trip? What did you do? What are you talking about?"

"Buchanons take care of their own. Hamilton isn't wanted here. We warned you to stay away from him."

So this was her fault?

"Dad, talk some sense into them. Beating people up is not the way to handle a problem. It's also not the way Buchanon Construction does business."

"No one said anything about beating him up." Brady flashed his teeth in a shark's grin. "We'll only have a chat and find out where he was last night."

"Allison's right on this one," her dad said. "You can't go off half-cocked and get yourselves tossed in jail. Let the police chief do his job. You did call Leroy, didn't you?"

Brady shook his head. "Not yet."

Dad pursed his lips and gave his son a scathing look.

"I'll call him, Dad." Allison moved into the U-shaped desk and reached for the phone. Jake was innocent. He wouldn't do anything as juvenile as vandalizing property. Would he?

While she reported the incident to the police, her brothers and dad murmured among themselves.

By the time she'd hung up, Jayla sailed through the door, carting her blender and a bag of groceries. She looked like a runway model with her sleek hair and well-dressed, superslim body. Allison's jeans and sweater felt dowdy.

When Jayla learned of the vandalism, she ground her teeth. Like Brady, Jayla could be a control freak who expected business to run smoothly all the time.

"Leroy is out today with a stomach virus, but Jerry is on duty and said he'd take look at the site," she told them.

"Good. We'll meet him there." Sawyer shoved the last bite of muffin in his mouth. Dawg watched with big, sad eyes.

Brady scored a muffin from Dawson's white sack and juggled it in his massive palm. To Allison, he said, "Do me a favor, okay?"

"What is it?" If he told her to stay away from Jake, she was going to hit him.

He reached in his pocket and pulled out a list. "I won't have time to do this now and I promised. Will you take a run to the supercenter and get this stuff for me?"

She frowned down at the long list of groceries and household supplies. "What's this for?"

He hitched a shoulder, his expression abashed. "Ah, you know."

Oh. Okay. She got it. Brady's heart was as big as the rest of him. He regularly bought groceries or gas or shoes or medicine for someone in need.

"Who's this week's recipient?"

"New family across the tracks. A woman and four kids."

Allison knew there was more to the story but didn't

push. Brady, for all his temper and bluster, was a soft touch like Mom.

"Should I deliver?"

"I'll take it by later. The mom's kind of embarrassed."

"Consider it done."

He leaned down and kissed the top of her head. "Are you getting shorter?"

She bopped him on the arm. He rubbed the spot and grinned. "Mosquito bite."

The men started for the door when Brady looked back at her. "One more thing."

She reached for a pen. "Did you leave something off the list?"

Brady narrowed his eyes. "Don't talk to loverboy about the vandalism until after the investigation."

Allison's heart sank. Just when she thought her brother was the best around, he kicked her in the gut. "Are you going to tell the police about your suspicions?"

Brady's mouth shrugged. "If he asks, I'll answer." And then he was gone, swaggering across the parking lot with his big heart and hard head directly at odds.

Allison showed up on his doorstep at the strangest times.

Jake was in Granny Pat's flower bed digging up something Florence called an apricot bearded iris. She wanted a start for her garden and he was the elected shovel man.

He leaned on the shovel handle and admired the little bit of woman tromping across the lawn, her dark, flyaway hair like wings.

"Are you lost?" He tipped back his hat. "It's ten in the morning. Shouldn't you be at work?"

"Perks of being family owned. What are you doing?"

She paused outside the flower bed, a messy thing that had gone wild in Granny Pat's absence.

"Digging. Want to help?" He was uncommonly happy to see her. Not that the Buchanons had scared him off. He wasn't scared. But in the time he had left in Gabriel's Crossing, he saw no point in making waves that might turn into a tsunami.

"Sure. What can I do?"

"When I dig, you get those little onion-looking things and put them in that bucket." He hitched his chin toward an empty white paint bucket.

"This is my mother's domain but I know my way around an iris."

He stuck his boot on the shovel and pushed. The rain-soft earth gave, emitting the scents of dying plants and fertile ground. He wiggled the spade carefully before levering up a clump of dirt and plant. "Are all women born with the flower gene?"

She reached into the dirt, heedless of getting her hands dirty. He admired that. A woman who wasn't afraid of dirt and work, two things he knew especially well.

"These are bulbs, not onions." She tapped the onion thing with a finger. "Lower the shovel into the bucket, dirt and all. No need to separate anything."

"You're brilliant."

"I am for a fact. Kind of late in the year to transplant irises. Who are these for?"

"Flo. She does things on her own timetable."

Allison stood and wiped her hands down the legs of her jeans. He was midtransfer when she said, "Take me to a movie tonight."

The clump of dirt hit the bucket with a sudden *thunk*. Where had that come from? Her brothers wanted to kill him and she wanted him to go to a movie?

He leaned the shovel against the side of the house. "Why?"

"Because I like you. We have fun together and I want to do something besides hang around your grandmother's house."

He didn't want to like the sound of that. "Not to spite your brothers?"

Her eyes met his and held. "Maybe a little. They had no right to confront you."

One of her strong suits was honesty. "I don't want to get between you and your family, Allison."

"Trust me, I know that. If you recall, I found that out the hard way a few years back. I don't always like your weird code of honor, but I appreciate the sentiment." She hoisted the bucket of iris bulbs, her focus on them. "I have to ask you something, Jake. Don't get mad, okay?"

"Starting a conversation that way is never a positive sign." He hunkered down beside the gaping hole in the ground and began to push dirt inside.

Allison set the bucket beside the porch and joined him, bringing along her honeysuckle scent. His heart began to misbehave.

"Someone vandalized a construction project last night."

His hand closed spasmodically on a gangly green stem. He tried not to let the implication sting. "You're asking if I had anything to do with damaging your family's work site?"

If he sounded incredulous, so be it.

"I don't want to."

He believed her. Those soft brown eyes were tormented as they held his with a plea.

"Will you believe me if I say no?"

"Yes."

With one small word and those big brown eyes, she had

the power to make him feel better. Let the others think what they wanted. As long as Allison believed in him, he was all right.

"I told you I'd never do anything to hurt you. Not if I could help it." The little disclaimer was self-preservation. If they got involved again, if he followed his heart instead of his head, they'd both end up hurt no matter his good intentions. Hurt he could handle. Another Buchanon disaster would be his demise. "What happened nine years ago was the product of a scared, angry kid. I'm not that boy anymore."

"Good. Then you can take me to a movie tonight like a grown man."

He snorted. "Somehow your logic confuses me."

"Do you know where my apartment is?"

She'd never told him where she lived, but he'd made it his business to find out. He was still rationalizing that one. "Sure. Why?"

"Pick me up at six forty-five, and we'll make the first showing at seven."

"What if I want to feed you dinner first?" Oh, man, he was wading into deep water.

Her face lit up. "Really?"

"I could use the break. Flo's been here every day, driving me nuts, running roughshod over both of us. She's even convinced Granny Pat to get out of the recliner and use the walker. And she slapped my hand for carrying Granny P. around like a baby." He patted dirt around the filled hole. "Flo claims I've been coddling my dear grandmother when she is perfectly capable of carting her own bones around."

Allison sat back on her heels and rubbed her forearm over her cheek. The action left a streak of dirt. "That's fabulous news."

"Yeah. I agree." Extra good news because he had a

rodeo coming up he desperately needed to enter and wanted Granny Pat up and around on her own before then. "Did you know Flo danced in Vegas?"

"Everybody knows that. The Daily Journal did an article on her." She put her dirty hands above her head and wiggled her fingers. "She danced with those giant feathered headpiece things."

"Exactly. Last night, she decided I should learn one of her routines. I was pathetic." He put his hands on his thighs and pushed to a stand. "I don't plan to repeat that performance tonight."

Allison popped up from the ground like a jack-in-the-box. "You danced with her?"

"I wouldn't call it dancing exactly. More like a trout caught in a fish net. Lots of flopping around."

"You never danced with me. And you owe me, buddy boy." She slapped an open palm on his chest. "I demand equal time."

"I just happen to have on my dancing boots!"

He grabbed her hands and began to sashay around the yard in a silly two-step. Allison stumbled on the edge of the concrete driveway but he easily held her up and kept dancing, scooting his boots on the fading grass and dipping her back and forth. He smiled at her laughter, enjoying the comfortable pleasure of her company, the ease with which they'd fallen back into old patterns of friendship, and this new something else that filled his chest with hope and made him pray for the impossible.

The memory of the dance that never happened was a heartbeat away, a bit of spun sugar that melted in the heat of his shame.

Enough. He was letting her get under his skin again. Or maybe still.

He whirled her up onto the postage stamp porch and

into the single lawn chair he'd put there himself for watching the sunsets.

"There you go. There's your dance. Paid in full."

Breathless, her cheeks flushed and pretty, her eyes sparkling, she shook her head. "Not good enough. I want music and a pretty dress and the whole banana. Come to Faith's wedding. Dance with me there for real."

The fun was spirited away on the heels of memory, a morning in November, a gunshot that should never have happened. He crouched on his toes in front of her. Taking her small hand in one of his rough ones, he said, "You're special to me, Allison."

"I know. And you're special to me. So come to the wedding. Show my brothers the man you've become. Show them you have nothing to hide."

"Are you still thinking about the vandalism?"

"Hiding out makes you look guilty."

He dropped her hand. "I don't hide."

"You avoid."

She had him there.

"Better than causing trouble."

"You have to forgive yourself, Jake," she said softly, her sweetness twisting him into a knot.

"I'm working on it." He pushed to a stand and turned his profile toward her, focusing across the street where a pair of puppies cavorted. Looking at Allison clouded his thinking.

She came up beside him, touched his arm with the tips of her fingers. Voice soft, she said, "Let go, Jake. Heal from this and move on."

Was it possible? Or was he fooling himself to think he'd ever come to that point? God had forgiven him, but he needed Quinn's forgiveness, too, before he could let go and forgive himself. And Quinn's forgiveness wasn't likely to happen in this lifetime.

He stepped off the porch and reached for the bucket of irises. "I told Flo I'd bring these over to her house."

"I have a lot more to say on this subject, Jake."

"Not today, okay?"

"Will you come to the wedding?"

"I'm thinking." He started toward his truck, parked on the cracked concrete drive. A clump of grass poked through the cracks.

"A cheap way to say no."

His shoulders lifted in a sigh. "I'm leaving now. Are you going or staying?"

"Going. With you." Allison shot him her ornery, Polly-anna grin that let him know she was coming along and there wasn't a thing he could do to stop her. As if he'd even try anymore. "How else can I tell you about all the work I've put in on this wedding? You need to see me in action to fully understand how *awesome* I am." She laughed and did a silly wiggle dance, letting him know she teased.

Jake rolled his eyes and groaned, but his mockery was all for show. Allison *was* awesome. The cute little cheer-leader had become a special lady. So special that he'd rather be stomped by a bull than see her sad.

But as long as she was a Buchanon, hurt was about the only outcome he could imagine.

Chapter Seven

Allison was nervous.

"You're being silly." She stood in front of a full-length mirror in her bedroom—the one Brady had hung on the back of the closet door—and assessed her outfit for tonight's movie date with Jake. She'd changed four times and now wondered if the skirt and heels were overkill. She was going out with Jake, for crying out loud, not Brad Pitt.

Allison looked in the mirror and saw the truth. She'd rather go with Jake.

Was she out of her mind? How else could she explain this twisted need to be with a man who'd rejected her once before and even now made no promise other than to leave her again?

She fluffed the sides of her hair. Her first official date with the grown-up Jake.

Impulsive. Foolish. And maybe stubborn enough to do the opposite of her brothers' demands. They were wrong about Jake.

As Mom always said, she led with her heart.

Allison grabbed the tail of her hot pink sweater, about to pull it over her head for one last change, when a knock sounded at the door. She yanked the sweater down again and peeked out the window at the black pickup in the duplex drive.

So much for changing her mind. She went to let him in.

"You're early."

He propped a hand on each side of the door facing. Oh, my. He looked really good. "I'm hungry."

"So you're all about the food? Thanks a lot. You're great for a girl's ego."

Green eyes danced. He pushed off from the door to gently tug her hair. "So needy."

She punched his arm. "Am not." But she was. Needy for him to be more than a friend, more than a guy she used to know.

Inside her small entry, a mere section of tile inside the front door, Jake removed his hat, a nicer one than he usually wore. "I like your place."

"Buchanon built to my specs. Jayla lives in the other side."

"I figured you for a girl who'd live with her parents until she married."

His comment about marriage offered the perfect opening. "When are you going to tell me about the woman in Wyoming?"

He gave her his most innocent look before his gaze dropped to her feet. "Aren't you going to wear shoes?"

"You can tell me, Jake. I won't judge. Remember how we could always tell each other anything."

Their long held secret buzzed in her ear like a gnat. She swatted it away.

"Not worth talking about. She and I didn't work out."

Didn't work out. Was that what he thought about the two of them? They hadn't worked out so he had chosen never to come home again?

"You look nice." He stepped close and his voice dipped low. "Smell good, too. Like flowers on the wind."

Allison's breath left her body. She reeled back in time to another voice, another man who'd said she smelled good.

But this was Jake. A man she'd trusted as much as her brothers. Mentally, she wrestled the other voice back inside her locked box and found safety in Jake Hamilton's green eyes.

Beneath the cowboy hat lived a good and godly man. Somehow she had to convince her brothers of that.

"Thanks for believing me," he said. "About the vandalism. I wouldn't."

"I know."

Expression soft as a cloud, he reached for a lock of her hair and gently tugged. For as far back as she could remember Jake had tugged her hair. Yet, tonight was different. The action held a deeper meaning, a new tenderness that resonated deep within her. His eyes questioned hers. He must wonder, as she did, where this subtle shift would take them—if it could, indeed, take them anywhere.

Warm and pleasant as a baby's breath, a tingle danced over Allison's skin. She didn't know what might happen between them if given the chance, but she believed in the impossible. God could mend the rift between her family and the only man who'd ever mattered.

Jake Hamilton held her heart in his cowboy hands— probably always had. As she'd trusted him that long ago night to hold her secret, she trusted Jake to hold her heart with care.

For the briefest, breath-held moment, she thought he might kiss her. Then, as if one of her brothers had tapped his shoulder, he dropped his hand and stepped back.

What would it take to push him over the edge, to break through the regret into the warm and tender center Allison knew existed? To a man who accepted responsibility for wrong, all the while holding a secret that could change attitudes?

Flummoxed and a little disappointed, she reverted to safer ground, a tease, a joke, meaningless chatter.

"Are you going to feed me or not?" Her voice was throaty and a little breathy, a dead giveaway for the emotion Jake didn't seem ready to handle.

One eyebrow flicked. "Persistent as a buffalo gnat."

His words teased but his eyes were serious. They'd walked into his emotional danger zone, and he didn't know what to do about it. Allison didn't either, though she wanted to go there and find out. Apparently, Jake didn't. At least, not yet.

She understood. He was the one carrying the baggage, not her.

Taking her tiny handbag from the end table by the love seat, Allison kept her tone light, though her heart rattled with hope and possibility. "Let's get this party started."

"Sounds good to me. I'm starved."

Jake guided her out into the faded day and used her key to lock the house. Against a bruised sky, the sun cast an orange glow along the horizon. There was little wind but the air had cooled into the November fifties, and Allison was glad for the heavy sweater she'd second-guessed.

"Chinese?" Jake asked. Safe topics. Food and weather.

"Perfect. Feed me now, feed me later." The old joke about Chinese food brought a smile and broke the lingering thread of emotion. He didn't want to discuss the feelings flowing between, couldn't face them, but he couldn't hide them either.

Side by side, they walked the short distance to his truck. When his hand lightly touched her back, Allison smiled.

Peanut oil. Jake recognized the smell inside the Chinese Buffet, a restaurant that hadn't existed when he and

Allison were in high school. Peanut oil and egg rolls and sweet and sour sauce. His belly did a happy dance.

It was either the smells or the crazy jitterbug he'd had all afternoon about this date. And then at her house. Man. He'd had the crazy urge to kiss her. He knew better. Knew he had no business making moves on Allison when he had nothing to offer but trouble and the memory of his tail-lights heading out of town.

But she looked amazing tonight. Gorgeous. He hadn't seen her dressed up in years and he liked the change. A lot. In jeans and sweater she knocked his hat in the dirt. In a skirt and heels, she blew all the common sense out of his head.

He had a lot more praying to do. They were playing with a powerfully combustive fire, and every time he stomped it out, Allison provided fresh fuel. She cared for him. He knew that. Knew and shuddered, both with dread and plea-sure. Nothing good could come of a romance with Allison Buchanon. Nothing.

Then why was he here? Why had he agreed to this movie date?

Sometimes a man was his own worst enemy.

With his hand against Allison's soft hot pink sweater, he guided her into the restaurant.

From behind a cash register next to the entrance a young Asian man nodded a greeting. Above his head a red-and-gold calendar written in Chinese hung next to a panda photo. The place was humming with customers, always a sign of good food.

The restaurant's one concession to the approaching holi-day was a tissue paper turkey above the buffet.

Beneath stainless-steel hoods, heat rose off the buffet in waves that reminded Jake of Allison's hair. But then, everything reminded him of Allison.

"Buffet or menu?" Jake asked.

Her pretty face creased in an ornery, Allison grin that made his heart light. She did that to him. Made him want things he didn't deserve and couldn't have.

"Oh, buffet, definitely," she said, "so we can try all the mysterious stuff."

"Chopsticks?" Jake reached into the cylinder and pulled out two pair. Chinese symbols decorated the red-papered sides.

"Are you kidding? I don't want to starve."

With a snort, he stuck the chopsticks in his shirt pocket. "Coward."

Grinning, they took their place in a busy line, and once they'd piled their plates to overflow and were seated, he quietly asked a blessing.

When he opened his eyes, Allison was watching him.

"What?" He touched his chin. "Do I have hot mustard on my face already?"

Her eyes went soft. "I love hearing you pray."

His insides spasmed. No one had ever said that to him. "Thanks."

He reached for his napkin, and self-conscious, made a display of shaking out the white square. His faith filled him with a peace he didn't understand, but he wasn't a preacher, not even close. He wasn't even that great at being a Christian, and he didn't deserve admiration.

"Any luck discovering who vandalized the property?"

"Not yet." Allison dipped an egg roll into duck sauce.

"The fearsome foursome still pointing at me?" He couldn't explain how much that had hurt, especially when history gave them reason to suspect him, but he'd fretted about the situation all day.

He reached for a wonton and crunched. Cream cheese. Not his favorite but he wasn't complaining.

"Not to my knowledge." She held the egg roll an inch from her lips. Pretty lips. He remembered how soft they were. How they trembled when she cried and how they tasted when she kissed. Like coconut. He dropped his gaze and fiddled with a pair of chopsticks. He shouldn't remember things like that.

"Can we please not talk about my family for one evening?" she asked.

Not that he could stop thinking about them or the shooting for one minute with her sitting across the table. "They're a part of you, Allison. A big part. Being with you brings everything back."

She touched the top of his hand with her fingertips. "I'm sorry. We have to find a way to move past all that."

"Why?"

"You know why."

His heart clattered like horse hooves against his rib cage. Coward that he was, he didn't ask what she meant. He was afraid she'd tell him.

To step away from the danger zone, Jake held up a bamboo skewer. "The teriyaki chicken is amazing. Want a bite?"

As soon as he asked, he wished he hadn't. Feeding her a bite of chicken was too personal, too romantic. Already, he could imagine the moment. Allison's lips close to his fingers. Watching her nibble the bite, her breath slipping like silk over his skin.

His insides shivered at the unwanted image.

This is the way he'd always feel if he let her close again. A mix of pleasure and pain fueled by a past that drew them together while simultaneously forcing them apart.

Thankfully oblivious to his random thoughts, Allison wiggled her index finger at something behind him. "Charity and the kids."

Great. Another Buchanon.

Jake twisted on the chair, wary, anxious. He didn't want Allison taking flack over a Chinese dinner. Her older sister came toward their table, and when Charity saw him, she smiled, an encouraging sign. Unlike their brothers, the Buchanon women had shown more pity than anger.

"Charity," he said, tipping his chin, though he couldn't bring himself to smile.

"Jake." Up close, he noted that her smile was strained and didn't reach her eyes. She wasn't glad to see him, but he understood that, too. He was trouble with a capital *T* as far as the Buchanons were concerned.

If Allison noticed the tension, she played dumb. As chipper as a Christmas elf, she tugged the children close to her chair. "These little dumplings are Ryan and Amber."

Amber dimpled up, a dark-eyed charmer already. Like her aunt, he thought.

"Are you a real cowboy?" she asked in that big-eyed innocent way of little kids.

"As real as they get, I guess."

"You ride bulls, don't ya?" Ryan, as blond as his mother but with freckles on his nose, looked vaguely familiar. Probably because of the photo Alison had shown him. He hoped that was all. Having a Buchanon kid mess with his bulls was the worst possible scenario.

"I try to."

"I'm going to ride bulls someday."

Jake's gut lurched.

"No, you are not." Charity scuffed his hair.

Expression mutinous, Ryan shrugged her off but didn't argue.

"Your mother's right, Ryan." Jake figured the least he could do was discourage the boy, just in case. "Bulls are dangerous animals. Even experienced guys like me get hurt."

"But you still ride."

The kid had him there. "Maybe I'm not too smart. A boy like you can go to college and make money without putting your life in danger."

"My dad has a dangerous job."

"Yeah, he does, for a lot better reason than money. I heard he's coming home soon."

"A little less than six months. A hundred and seventy-one days to be exact." Charity offered a genuine smile this time. "But who's counting." She put her hands on Ryan's shoulders. "Come on, kids. Let's find a table or we'll be late to the football game." She looked to Allison. "Are you going? The Bears and the Tigers are a big rivalry and this is the season ender. Tonight is win, lose or go home until next year."

Jake's teriyaki soured in his stomach. He'd seen the Beat the Bears and All the Way to State signs slathered on the store windows with white shoe polish.

"Movie night for us. You all have fun." Allison bent forward and smacked a kiss on Amber's cheek. "Love you, princess. You, too, Ryan, though I know you'll gag if I kiss you in public."

Ryan made a gagging noise with a hand to his throat.

Charity hooked an elbow around his neck and as she led him away, she looked at Allison and said, "Could I see you for a minute? Privately?" She jerked her chin slightly away from the table.

Allison glanced at Jake before laying her napkin aside. "Be right back."

Jake watched her sister lead her a few steps away, studied the intensity of the brief conversation before Allison returned to the table.

Retaking her seat, she avoided his gaze. He was no fool. Charity, the polite, didn't like seeing her sister with Jake Hamilton.

"What was that about?"

Allison dipped the end of a half-eaten egg roll into plum sauce and stirred it around.

"Nothing important."

"You were never a good liar. She was upset about me being here with you. Wasn't she?"

Allison's glance flicked to him and then to her eggroll. "We agreed not to discuss my family tonight. Remember?"

He remembered. But his appetite was gone.

Trying to avoid Buchanons didn't work. They were everywhere.

The movie was a real snoozer and the theater all but empty thanks to the football game. Allison and Jake spent most of the ninety minutes imitating the bad dialogue and mocking the overly dramatic story line. The rest of the time, they fed each other popcorn they didn't want and tried to pretend that sitting together in the dark theater wasn't a bit romantic.

The trouble was, the only other couple in the theater sat down front and used their ninety minutes as a make-out session. Once Jake murmured, "Get a room, Romeo," and set Allison off into a fit of muffled giggles. She laughed even harder when Jake put his hand over her mouth and in a stage whisper said, "Shh. Be quiet. Those people are trying to watch the movie."

Later, when they left the theater, Jake looped an arm around her shoulders and said, "That's the best show I've seen in a long time. Thanks for making me go."

"Are you crazy? It was terrible."

"I'm talking about the show down front, not the movie." He bumped her with his side and grinned.

Her belly did a flip-flop. "I had fun."

"Me, too."

Allison was relieved to hear it. The brief and terse exchange with Charity could have ruined the evening. Afterward, Jake had gone quiet and moody for a while.

Thankfully, the awful movie and ridiculous public display of affection down front had changed the mood to light and easy.

They sauntered down the sidewalk in front of the theater past the darkened storefronts. Other than a couple of convenience stores off First Street, Gabriel's Crossing closed up at night. A few cars puttered by including the local police car making rounds. Allison lifted her hand and waved. Jerry was a good friend of Dawson's which made him a friend of every Buchanon. The officer waved back and gave a soft honk.

Allison stopped in front of the Texas Rose Boutique, a shop of girly things and flowers owned by one of her friends, but then everyone was a friend in Gabriel's Crossing. Almost everyone.

In front of a snowy background, two flocked trees filled one corner of the show window. In the other, Angela had stacks of gaily-wrapped gifts, each with a product from the shop on top. Purses, perfume, scarves.

"The stores are already decorating for Christmas."

"Too early. We haven't had Thanksgiving yet."

"It's this way every year. Christmas crowding out Thanksgiving when we all have so much to be thankful for," she said. "What are you and Miss Pat planning for Thanksgiving?"

They stood side by side, peering into the pretty display.

With his arm still casually slung across her shoulder, she could feel his warmth through his jacket. "No plans yet."

She wanted to invite him to the Buchanon feast. Instead, she said, "Maybe I could come over and help you cook."

He chuffed. "Help me? You'd have to cook everything except mashed potatoes. I've got those down."

She bumped his side. "Thanks to me. So what do you say? Thanksgiving night? I'll come over."

"What about your family dinner?"

"At noon. Mom's a stickler. Stuff your faces before you watch the Cowboys and the Lions."

Their breath made fog circles on the windowpane while Allison awaited his reply.

"I thought you'd jump at my offer."

He turned his face toward hers. "Can I get back to you on that?"

A frisson of disappointment dampened her mood. "Sure. No big deal."

The invitation, like Faith's wedding, was a very big deal. She wanted to spend Thanksgiving with him. But the ball was in his court.

They started on down the darkened sidewalk, pausing often to peek inside a window or chuckle at some outrageous item on display.

As they turned the corner, heading toward the parked truck, a yellow-white streetlight washed the sidewalk in shiny shadows. Hers and Jake's stretched out like dark clowns on stilts. In shadow was the only time she looked tall, a sight that never failed to amuse her.

Jake's hand slipped from her shoulder. Allison considered reaching for his hand beneath the cover of darkness, but she didn't. Jake had to find his own way in this relationship, as she had.

The damp scent rising from the distant Red River mingled with the chill of autumn. A half-dozen blocks south, the high school marching band played the Tigers' fight song, and Allison was almost certain she smelled grilled hot dogs.

She turned her head toward the music and the tall football lights visible from First Street.

Beside her, Jake was silent. The town's mania for high school football had ostracized him as a teen. No wonder he avoided conversation about the sport he'd once played with as much passion as her brothers.

He stared in that direction, his profile serious.

Feeling tender and sorry, she slipped her hand into his, a touch of comfort. When he glanced at her, questioning, she squeezed his fingers. His skin was rough, his grip strong, as he squeezed back. No words were needed.

Her heels tapped quietly on the bricks as they crossed the street.

Once inside the truck, Allison clicked on the CD player. The mood had shifted in that short walk from movie to vehicle. She couldn't quite put her finger on the emotion, but the feelings hovered in the warm cab and struck them both silent. Sadness, longing, regret, but something else, too.

With the heater at her feet and the CD filling in for conversation, they rode the few blocks to her apartment.

One hand on the door lever, Allison prepared to hop out with a cheery wave and a hearty thanks, but Jake killed the engine and got out, coming around to her door.

The step up into the cab was high for anyone but especially someone vertically challenged like Allison. Jake took her elbow and she jumped to the ground with a short laugh.

The corner streetlight cast pale light on her small front lawn, enough to maneuver to the doorway.

"I can walk to the door by myself."

"I know." But he walked her there anyway. His boots made soft padding sounds while her heels stabbed holes in the ground. Heels for a movie. What had she been thinking?

"Well," she said, "thank you for the fantastic Chinese and a stellar film."

She expected him to make some remark about being hungry again or about the awful movie, but he didn't. Instead, he gazed down at her in the darkness, his face in shadowy relief, quiet again.

"What are you thinking about?" She didn't know why she bothered to ask. No male she'd ever known wanted to answer that question.

"You're something."

"So I've been told, though not in quite that tone."

His lips curved, and she was sure he moved a little closer though how he could get any closer on the small square slab of concrete porch seemed impossible.

"I wish—"

She touched his mouth with her fingertips. "No wishes. Reality is better."

He captured her fingers and pulled them away from his warm mouth, holding them against his chest. He stared, head bent, sheltering her with the brim of his hat. He was close enough that she felt his warm breath against her face. Longing rose in her throat, trapped there by a past they couldn't remedy.

His cowboy-rough fingertips stroked her cheek. His face moved closer. But then he kissed her on the forehead and stepped away.

"Night, Allison."

Before Allison could regain her composure and kick him in the shin, he stepped off the porch and strode away, leaving her in the dark.

Chapter Eight

Jake kicked himself all the way home and for the next couple of days, but no matter how much self-recrimination he heaped upon his Stetson, Allison was like a sweet perfume he couldn't wash off his shirt. Regardless of what he was doing, he thought about her.

As if that wasn't making him completely insane, every evening she popped in to see Granny Pat. And him. And every evening, he fought like a tiger to keep his distance. Still, she lingered, impressing him with her ability to make chicken dumplings that Granny Pat craved or convincing him to watch a sappy Hallmark movie that left him with a hot air balloon in his chest.

Matters got worse on Friday when he ducked into the drugstore for Granny Pat's prescription refill only to run into Allison's best friend. Faith, the long of it, was loaded down with sunscreen, lotions, cosmetics and a lot of other girly stuff.

"For Saint Thomas," she'd told Jake with a happy smile, a statement that led directly to the wedding and an effort to extract a promise that Jake would be there. He'd stuttered around and left the store without a commitment but the date and time were imprinted behind his eyeballs like a scene from a movie—a cross between Cinderella and a horror flick. Allison would be the beautiful princess. Her brothers would inflict the horror. And Jake Hamilton would be the bad guy who ruined the entire affair for everyone.

Better to skip the ordeal.

But when the Saturday of the wedding rolled around, he was restless as a red ant.

"What is wrong with you, Jacob?" Granny Pat sat in her chair knitting like a mad woman. The *click-clack* of needles was driving him crazy.

"Nothing."

Granny Pat made a huffing noise. "Who was that on the phone? Your woman in Wyoming?"

He scowled. "Bill Brown in Denton. We travel together some."

"Guess he wants to know when you're getting back in the game?"

"I'm not worried about it." No use worrying at this point. The die was cast. He was basically broke. "The fall rodeos are winding down."

"What *are* you worried about? Allison Buchanon and her big, burly brothers?"

He gave her a cool look. "Some things are better left alone, Granny P."

"Umm-hmm. Tell that to Allison." *Click-clack. Click-clack. Click-clack.* The needle speed increased. If she could move the rest of her as fast as she moved those needles, she'd be in the Olympics. Suddenly, the click-clacking stopped. She rested the wad of knitting in her lap. "Your grandpa wants you to know something, son."

Grandpa again.

"Sometimes a man has to step up to the plate and be a man even when he isn't sure."

"What's that supposed to mean?"

She picked up the knitting again. "Beats me. Ask Ralph. He said it."

Jake barked a short laugh. "I need to go somewhere." Anywhere.

"That's what Ralph said. Tell the boy to go on. Things can't get much worse and sometimes they get better."

Was she talking about the wedding? Ralph or not, she was right. Things couldn't get much worse with the Buchanons. So what if he showed up at the wedding long enough to give Allison a dance he'd owed her since high school and to offer his congratulations to the happy couple? What's the worst thing that could happen?

At that point, he got stuck. The worst thing would be ruining Faith's wedding.

But the Buchanons wouldn't do that. Would they? They loved Faith, and they loved their sister. Allison had thrown her heart and passion into planning a perfect day for her best friend. The brothers might seethe but they wouldn't cause a scene.

He bent to kiss his grandmother on the papery cheek. "Is Flo coming over?"

"I don't need a babysitter, Jacob. As much as I don't like toddling around on this walker like an old lady, I can if I have to. Go to the wedding. Take that gift on my dresser."

"You bought a gift?"

"Faith sent me an invitation so I asked Maggie Thompson to bring something over from her shop." Granny's face went nostalgic. "I remember when Faith used to ride her bike up here and I'd give her homemade cookies and let her talk about her daddy. That was after the divorce when she was hurting bad. Her mama was, too, but she was so busy trying to make a living for the two of them and hang on to her house. I know a little about that kind of worry. Bless her heart."

"I never knew we were in danger of losing our property."

"We've had some bumps in the road, but Ralph thinks something will turn up."

Jake was playing mental gymnastics. "Are we talking about then or now?"

Her needles paused. "Both. But don't worry. I'll handle Ned Butterman and his bank."

With a sick feeling, Jake asked, "You mortgaged the house?"

She waved a hand. "A while back. Before that silly fall. I needed a little cash. You were riding in Vegas and I wanted to be there."

"Vegas was four years ago. And I paid your way. I bought the tickets."

Granny Pat gave him the look of idiocy. "Jacob, I was in Vegas. I had to try my luck."

Jake's head fell back. He stared up at the hand-plastered ceiling. A thin crack ran from one corner to the light fixture. "You mortgaged the house for gambling money? Why didn't you tell me? This house means everything to you. That's the reason I brought you home!"

And the reason he'd been willing to deal with the Buchanons as long as necessary to see her well again.

"That's why I wanted to come home. I wanted to be here as long as I can. Before—" she sniffed "—well, you know."

"This is not happening." He rammed a hand across the top of his head. "I will not let you lose this house."

"You're a dear, good boy, but money doesn't grow on trees."

True. His money grew on grass. He swallowed thickly. His one asset was his bulls.

"How bad is it?" he asked grimly.

"I told you not to fret."

"How bad, Granny Pat?"

At his harsh tone, she looked him in the eye. "I have

until after the first of the year to come up with the money. Ned doesn't foreclose during the holidays, which I think is mighty nice of him."

Foreclosure. Lord, help them both. "Exactly how do you think you can come up with that kind of money?"

"I buy lottery tickets every week."

Jake groaned. "Granny Pat!"

She rolled her eyes. "I'm joking. I learned my lesson on gambling. The truth is I don't know where I'll find the money." Her bottom lip trembled. "I don't want to go to the nursing home."

His grandmother's frightened, vulnerable expression jabbed at him. Jake took up her hairbrush and ran the bristles gently through her cloud of white hair. "You're not going to a nursing home." No matter what he had to do. "If worse comes to worse, you'll live with me."

"Darling boy, think on that. You're on the road most of the time. Besides, I don't want to leave Gabriel's Crossing. We're the last of the Hamiltons. We started this town, and this is where I plan to end."

The feathery wisps of white hair sifted through his fingers. *Aw, Granny.* Why hadn't she told him?

More than ever, he needed to work, but ranching and rodeo was all he knew. Manny would hire him in a heartbeat but that would lock him into Gabriel's Crossing.

All he had left were his bulls.

Not his bulls. Anything but that.

Granny Pat reached up and placed a white, spotted hand on his, stopping the motion of the brush. "You go on to Faith's wedding. Standing there worrying won't fix a thing."

"I'm not going." He put the brush on the end table.

"Yes, you are. Faith Evans is our friend, sweet as syrup, and never once turned her back or judged you when Quinn got hurt. The least you can do is put on your Sunday best and honor her wedding day."

Her words struck Jake like a cold rain in the face. He was as self-focused as a mule. This wedding wasn't about him. It wasn't even about Allison, though she played a big part in the day. Today was for Faith and her friends and family. "Tell you what. I'll go to the wedding if you'll go with me."

She put a hand to her cheek, her eyes wide. "Oh, Jacob, I don't know. Look at me."

"No excuses. You want to, and we owe it to Faith."

Granny tossed her skein of yarn into a basket at her side. "Well, I'm sick and tired of this house, I tell you for sure. I'd like nothing better today than to see Faith married to her Prince Charming."

"Then you're going." And so was he. Faith was a friend and a longtime neighbor, and the Hamiltons didn't ignore something as important as a friend's wedding. Even if Ned Butterman and all the Buchanons in Texas showed up.

Allison was halfway down the aisle of Jesus Our Savior Church when she saw him. Pachelbel's "Canon in D" faded though she managed to keep moving, past the swags of white tulle and kissing pomanders festooning the aisles in Thanksgiving colors.

Jake had come. She kept her eyes forward on the groom and his attendants, the flower girls and ring bearers, but her whole being wanted to do a happy dance down the aisle.

Nothing like making a fool of yourself at your best friend's wedding.

Her chiffon formal stirred around her heels in a swishing sound. She suddenly felt like a princess.

After taking her place across from the best man, Allison watched the bridesmaids file in exactly the way she'd rehearsed them. Then the organist launched into Wagner's "Here Comes the Bride," and the guests rose. Cameras flashed and the guests' collective sigh filled Allison's heart with pride and her eyes with tears. An elegantly beautiful Faith floated down the aisle of her childhood church on the arm of her grandfather, the only man in her life until now. Until Derrick.

Allison glanced toward the groom. Though he nervously swallowed, his eyes blazed with love for his bride. He smiled and Faith's answering radiance was all the pay Allison would ever want for coordinating this perfect day for them.

Someday she wanted a wedding like this with a groom who looked at her with the future in his eyes. A man and woman so in love that they saw only each other in this crowd of well-wishers.

Love was a beautiful gift that bathed the small church in an aura of light and hope. She wanted that with all her heart.

Teary and joyful, Allison glanced toward Jake again. She hadn't meant to, but her heart squeezed at the endearing sight of the cowboy in jeans and brown sport coat standing behind his grandmother's wheelchair. He'd brought Miss Pat.

Expression serious, his focus remained on the bride and groom. As hers should be.

He'd come. She couldn't get that thought out of her head. In spite of everything, he'd come.

She looked toward the pew filled with Buchanons. Mom and Jayla dabbed at their eyes while Charity whispered something to a restless Amber. The Buchanon men filled the rest of the pew like the front line of the Dallas Cowboys. Gorgeous, powerful, wonderful men with heads as hard as bricks.

They had better behave themselves.

Jake remembered why he didn't like weddings. They made him feel things he didn't want to think about. Bulls he understood. Rodeos, too. But weddings and relationships baffled him, filled his chest with a strange heat, like heartburn to the max.

He'd known Allison would look pretty, but he hadn't expected all the air to rush out of him like a deflated balloon. In a long dress the color of mint ice cream with her dark hair swept up on the side and held by a golden-orange flower, she'd knocked his eyes out. But then, the old guilt had returned with a sledgehammer to the brain, reminding him of the party he'd missed, of the promised dance he'd failed to deliver.

Failures. So many, and now he'd failed Granny Pat by not realizing sooner that the once strong independent woman needed his help in more ways than one. He didn't know what he was going to do about the mortgage. The worry rolled round and round in his brain and had no answer. For today he shelved the mortgage along with the many other problems and failures. Gabriel's Crossing made him feel like the worst failure on earth. No wonder he had stayed away.

When the emotional ceremony ended and guests moved like one body into the reception hall, he found a quiet corner to park Granny Pat's chair and make himself scarce. If the Buchanons had noticed him, none had reacted. So far. Might as well not press his luck since he was batting zero lately.

The reception hall was decked out like a New England foliage tour. Rusts and golds, oranges and yellows mingled with the mint green. In another rush of color, the attendants and the bride and groom came through the double doors to cheers and applause.

"Isn't she the prettiest thing?" Granny Pat said when Faith and her groom stepped behind a table to cut the three-tiered cake.

"Can't argue with that," Jake said, but he turned his gaze toward Allison as she crossed the room to hug her best friend. She looked as happy as the bride, a thought that generated mental pictures of Allison in a white gown standing beneath a lighted arch with candles flickering. She was the marrying kind of girl, and he questioned the manhood of every male in Gabriel's Crossing for not snatching her up. If she was married, he could stop thinking about her. He'd have to.

Cameras clicked and flashed, and a videographer panned the room before focusing on the fancy-looking cake table. Once the cake was cut, the newlyweds moved out onto the dance floor for the first dance. A romantic "Can't Help Falling in Love" swept them around the room, their eyes locked on each other in a way that kept the rest of the world out. Jake got that hot air balloon feeling in his chest again.

Granny Pat tapped his hand. "Get us some punch, Jacob. And some of those appetizers."

Relieved to have something to do, he left his grandmother talking to the postmistress and made his way toward the nearest table.

"Punch or mulled cider?" a smiling young lady asked, indicating a tiny glass cup that couldn't contain more than a swallow of liquid.

"One of each," he said to the woman who, like all the others manning the cake and drinks and appetizers, wore autumn colors. Jake gestured toward the corner. "One for my grandmother."

"Oh, that is so thoughtful. You brought your grandma."

"She brought me," he said ruefully.

The woman smiled. "You're Jake, aren't you?"

"That's right. You look familiar."

Her smile widened. "I should. We lived across the street from you when I was in grade school."

He pointed at her. "You're Maddie?"

She laughed. "I might have changed a little."

A little was a major understatement. She'd been around eight years old with big teeth and skinned knees. "You were about this high when you moved away."

"Now I've moved back, and so have you."

"Just visiting."

She tilted her head with a smile. "Too bad. But maybe we can dance later?"

The question caught him off guard. Was little Maddie coming on to him? "I'm not much of a dancer, but thanks for asking."

He would only dance once, and only with Allison.

Before the conversation could go somewhere uncomfortable, Jake took the miniature cups and went for the appetizers. He approached the table from one direction in time to see Quinn Buchanon approach from the other. Their eyes connected. Quinn's narrowed into a glare. His chiseled jaw hardened.

Jake got that sinking feeling, as if he'd been tossed over the head of a rank bull. He had plenty of reason to be at this wedding, but for Faith's sake, he wanted no trouble.

The sandy blond Quinn looked fit and strong in a black suit that hid his weaker arm. But Jake knew the damage was there. With a tight chin dip, he pivoted away from the appetizers and back to his grandmother on the periphery of the dance floor behind the food tables.

He handed her the punch.

"Where's my snack?" She sipped at the cup.

"Later."

One white eyebrow lifted. "Hamiltons don't wimp out."

He didn't ask her meaning. Granny Pat didn't miss much of anything.

By now, other pairs had moved onto the dance floor. "Are you ready to go yet?"

"No, I am not. After being stuck in that prison for months, I'm ready to kick up my heels." She tilted her face toward him. "If I don't starve to death first."

"You'll get your plate of food."

"And cake, too. Lots of icing with some of those pillowy mint things." She patted his hand where he held the wheelchair. "Go on, now. Remember what your grandpa said. Be a man."

"Were you always a troublemaker?"

She shot him an ornery grin as he once more wove his way through the people. His elbow bumped Allison's nephew, who looked miserable in a snazzy tux with his hair slicked to one side. Jake empathized. No eleven-year-old boy wanted to be trussed up like a penguin.

"Hi, Jake."

Surprised that the kid remembered his name, Jake paused. "Ryan, right? Nice duds."

Ryan tugged at his tie. "Mom made me wear this. I'm choking to death."

"I feel your pain."

"Bull riders don't have to dress up if they don't want to."

"Not much call for fancy clothes in the rodeo."

"Yeah, another good reason to ride bulls."

Jake saw an opportunity and took it. "Was that you the other day at Manny Morales's ranch?"

Ryan's eyes widened. "When?"

"Look, Ryan, if that was you, stay clear of those bulls. You can get hurt."

The boy's expression closed up. "I don't know what you're talking about. I gotta go."

With an inward sigh, Jake snagged a couple of plates and piled them high with food, paying little attention to his selections. Maybe he was wrong. Maybe Ryan wasn't the right kid.

A few old pals spotted him and stopped to talk, a nice moment that elevated his mood and made him glad he'd come. Les and Thad invited him to a fishing tourney. Some folks in Gabriel's Crossing had apparently forgotten his ugly past.

By the time he reached his grandmother again, he decided he'd made the right decision by attending the wedding. Things were going pretty well. Even the encounter with Quinn.

Granny Pat took the plate of food and balanced the fancy white china on her lap. "I could use more punch."

"I'm not making another trip, Granny. If you want food, we have a freezer full of casseroles."

She pointed a crooked index finger toward the floor. "That boy sure is cozy with your woman."

"I don't have a wo—" The word left his brain. The best man, a lean blond with a big smile and perfect teeth, held Allison in his arms. Taller than her by several inches, the blond guy held her in the usual way, nothing suggestive, but the look in his eyes and the smile on Allison's face started a slow burn in Jake's gut.

His grip tightened on his plate. Even though he thought Allison was the marrying kind of girl, he didn't want to watch her dance with some other guy. Yet, he couldn't take his eyes off them either. Allison's dress floated around her like a puff of mint smoke, a cotton candy fairy tale. The man said something and she laughed. Jake couldn't hear her, but he saw the flash of teeth and the cute way she tipped her chin up and squinted her brown eyes.

His gut clenched into a hard knot.

Mr. Best Man tightened his hold on Allison's waist.

Jake set his untouched plate of food aside.

When the other man pulled Allison's hand against his chest, Jake had seen enough. He owed her a dance. Time to pay up.

He was on the dance floor before his brain had time to think things through. He tapped Best Man on the shoulder. "I'm cutting in."

Best Man looked to Allison who nodded. "We'll dance later, Brian. Okay?"

Jake's back teeth ground together. Brian needed to stick his head in the punch bowl.

"Count on it." The tuxedoed blond gave Allison another of his dazzling smiles and evaporated from sight. Jake imagined him with green punch dripping down his face.

Allison tipped her head to one side and held out her arms. "It's about time."

Jake swept her into the dance, determined to maintain a respectable distance, to get this long-promised dance out of the way and hit the road. At least that's what he told himself. This dance was her idea. He hadn't even wanted to come.

"You look beautiful." He didn't know where the words came from. He hadn't meant to say them.

She beamed, and the smile she gave him radiated far more wattage than the one she'd given Brian. "My dress for the graduation dance was pink."

"I didn't want to stand you up that night."

"I know."

He doubted if she knew the full story but it was like Allison to simply forgive him and move on, to give him the benefit of the doubt. He wished her brothers had the same attitude.

"I thought leaving was the best thing I could do under the circumstances." He'd been young and heartbroken, and the months of finishing high school with the whole town mourning the loss of Quinn's golden arm had taken a terrible toll on his soul. He'd been shunned, beaten up and hated. Rodeo provided a much-needed escape, and he'd wimped out the night of the graduation dance to avoid more conflict. "I took the coward's way out."

"Life wasn't easy for you back then."

No, but life hadn't been easy for Quinn either. Or for any of the Buchanons. "Quinn looks good."

"Stop worrying about him."

Like that would ever happen.

He wrapped his hand around Allison's small fingers and pulled them against his heart. If blond Brian could do that, so could he. "You and me. We would never have worked out."

She gave him a long, sad look, and then laid her head on his shoulder. Her dark hair tickled the side of his neck, and he caught a whiff of the flowers in her hair…and cake icing, sweet and delicious.

His heart gave one giant *kaboom.*

Lord, help him. He'd fooled himself to think he could ever forget his little champion, his best cheerleader, this special girl who'd grown into an incredible woman.

He swirled her around the floor, as conflicted as he'd ever been and painfully aware that he was not doing her a favor.

One dance. One dance, and he was out of here.

His hand tightened on her waist. He wasn't about to pull her closer though the man in him wanted to.

She was such a tiny woman. Holding her made him feel manly and strong.

Couples bumped against them but Jake paid them no mind. He was too busy trying to keep his thoughts in order. From the dais, a band played "The Way You Look Tonight."

Beautiful. She looked so beautiful.

He kept telling himself he'd be glad when the song ended, but he was lying.

Someone tapped him on the shoulder. "Taking over, pal. I think you need to leave."

Allison raised her head. "Sawyer, go away."

Quinn appeared beside his brother. "Dance with Sawyer, little sister."

"I am dancing. Get lost."

But Jake loosened his hold and stepped back from her. He'd promised no trouble and he was keeping that promise. "Thanks for the dance, Allison."

"But—"

Sawyer grabbed Allison and spun her away, though he could hear her protesting before she disappeared in a swirl of mint green into the sea of wedding guests.

Jake's fist tightened. "I'm getting tired of your attitude, Quinn."

"Want to take it outside? Or are you afraid to hit a cripple?"

Karen Buchanon appeared next to her son. Her voice was low and conversational but held enough steel to get Quinn's attention. "Cool it, right now. This is Faith's wedding and you big lugs are not going to create a scene. You hear me?"

She shot her son a smile that, to the onlooker, appeared warm, but Jake saw the warning. Apparently, so did Quinn. He eased back, but his glare remained on Jake.

Everything in Jake wanted to resist. But he glanced at Quinn's right arm and then into Karen's concerned face and made his decision.

"Don't worry, Mrs. B. I won't cause a problem. I'm leaving."

She put long-nailed fingers on his elbow. "Thank you, Jake. Some things are for the best."

He'd been telling Allison that for weeks.

As he walked away from the dance floor and back to Granny P., he searched the hall for a small brunette in foamy green. He didn't see her. For the best, like Karen said. A man didn't start something he couldn't finish.

But Jake was tired of backing down, tired of turning the other cheek, tired of looking like a coward. Was this what it meant to be a Christian? Always slinking away with his tail tucked between his legs?

He took hold of Granny Pat's wheelchair and, with his jaw tight enough to crack iron, rolled her out into the evening.

Allison put on a happy face for the remainder of the reception but inside she seethed. After Faith and Derrick rushed out of the building amid a hail of birdseed and bubbles and into a waiting limo, she let the repressed tears slide down her cheeks. Everyone thought she was crying with happiness for her best friend. She was. But she was also crying for the incomplete dance, for the idiots she called brothers, and for Jake.

She slashed at the tears with the back of her hand. Someone offered a hankie. Through blurry eyes, she saw Brady.

"You're a jerk," she said.

"What did I do?"

"You know."

"That narrows it down." He put his powerful arms around her in a brotherly hug and lifted her off the floor like a child. "The wedding turned out great."

She sniffed. "Thanks."

He put her down. "I'm proud of you, sis."

"Then stay out of my life."

His blue eyes regarded her with something akin to sympathy. "So, that's what this is all about?"

"You had no right."

He held up both palms in surrender. "I didn't."

"You would have."

"True." He snagged a bottle of bubbles from a linen-covered table and blew through the wand. Iridescent bubbles glinted beneath the lights, now on in full power. "We're all heading over to Mom and Dad's later. The twins are bringing Bailey and Kristin. You coming?"

The twins always had girls on their arms. Usually a different one each time. "I have to finish up here."

"I could help out. Keep you company."

Allison looked at her brother with a mix of frustration and adoration. Brady, the big brother who'd carried her piggyback across mud puddles and up hills. The brother who'd taught her to ride a bike and to count by fives. He'd always been there for her. Until Jake.

Blood is thicker than water. The Buchanon way. Buchanons stick together.

Thoughts of Jake and their half dance crowded in.

But Jake had walked away and left her. Again.

Chapter Nine

Days later, Jake couldn't stop worrying about the wedding fiasco. He was glad he hadn't caused a scene but the Buchanons' attitude rankled him no end. He was a man, no longer a teenage kid they could kick to the curb. Worse, he couldn't get Allison and their slow dance out of his memory. Her soft skin. Her flippy, flower-scented hair. Her sparkly laugh that hit him right in the center of his chest.

With Allison, he lost his ability to reason. He didn't know what to do.

The longer he remained in Gabriel's Crossing, the more of a problem she would become. But he couldn't leave either. Granny had him in a serious bind, and he would not let her lose the house. No matter what he had to do. Though after speaking to the banker, he had come away more concerned than ever.

Maybe this was God's way of getting him to pray more. For sure, he'd done plenty of talking to the Lord since the moment he'd come home to Gabriel's Crossing. Take the issue with Quinn and the Buchanons. If God intended him to suffer for his wrongs, He was succeeding. Granny, the house, Quinn and Allison. All of them kept him way more humble than he'd ever thought necessary.

If he wasn't with Allison, he missed her. Knowing she was in the same town, only a few blocks away, had him driving by her apartment like some lovesick cowboy even when he knew she was at work.

But he didn't love her. Couldn't. She deserved a man who wouldn't come between her and the family she adored. A man who could live in her town with his head held high, a man she and others respected, a man who wasn't growing poorer by the minute.

From the living room, he heard his grandmother's laughter, a good sound. She was getting better and that was worth everything and anything he had to endure.

Florence came over nearly every day to tease and cajole his grandmother onto her feet. She offered to teach Granny Pat to dance and mentioned a gig on *Dancing with the Stars*. Between Flo and Allison, his grandmother was bound to get better.

"Don't they hire celebrities for the TV show?" Jake asked as he sauntered into the living room, sipping a glass of orange juice.

Flo waved away his concerns. "I still have contacts in the business."

"I talked to Ralph about this crazy idea of yours, Flo," Granny said. "He says you're full of beans."

Flo laughed her bawdy laugh and pushed at her mile-high platinum-blond hair. Jake could imagine her dancing with fruit on her head and a train of feathers swishing behind her high heels, those long legs prancing around a stage with other over-the-top women. Granny's age, Flo's love of cosmetic surgery put her twenty years younger. He couldn't imagine Flo being anyone's granny.

"Maybe I am, but if not Hollywood, we'll head to Mexico. A cruise in the sun is what you need."

"I've always wanted to go on a cruise."

"Then, get your skinny self out of that chair." Flo whipped the throw from Granny's lap. "Quit acting like an old lady. You told me yourself the docs saw no reason why you weren't on your feet."

"Ralph and I had other things to take care of."

"Such as?"

"We'll talk later." Granny Pat cut a glance toward Jake who was folding a basket of towels on the couch. "Jacob, don't you have somewhere to go? I tell you, Flo, the boy has no social life. We fixed him up with that bouncy little Allison and he refuses to take the bait."

Jake's fingers tightened on his condensing glass. That bouncy little Allison. "Who fixed me up?"

"Ralph and me. I told you about that, but Ralph says we'll need dynamite to get you moving."

"Tell Ralph I have a life and I have a career that keeps me busy." He couldn't believe he'd responded to a figment of his grandmother's imagination. Again. "But you come first. If you want me out of your hair, you'll get well."

"She's going to dance, I tell you." Flo did a little soft-shoe with hands out to her sides. She was still good.

"You must have been something in your day."

She chucked him under the chin with a wink. "Still am, buddy boy. Now, if you have somewhere else to go, I'll be here all afternoon. Pat and I are going to plan a cruise, finish knitting that pile of yarn and talk about men. You don't want to be here for that."

He recognized a brush-off when he got one. "I'm headed out to Manny's to ride some practice bulls anyway." He downed the juice and clinked the glass on the coffee table. "I have my cell. Call if you need anything."

Granny Pat flapped her fingers at him. "We'll be fine. Don't stay out too late."

Smiling at a command he hadn't heard in years, he put on his hat and headed out the door.

He had more in mind than riding bulls today, but

Granny didn't need to know his decision yet. He would ask Manny for a job on the ranch to supplement the weekend rodeos. If that meant sticking around Gabriel's Crossing a while longer, he would.

Somehow he'd keep Allison and her family out of the picture. Once the Hamilton house debt was resolved, he could kiss Gabriel's Crossing goodbye. Maybe by spring.

At the Double M Ranch, he'd parked and started toward the barn when Paulina's voice turned him around. She came out the back door and hurried toward him, urgency in her movements.

He went on alert. Something was wrong.

"Jake," she cried. "I try to call you. Where you been?"

He pulled out his cell and saw two missed calls. How did that happen? "What's wrong?"

"Manny. The big white bull pinned him."

Adrenaline jacked into Jake's bloodstream. The big white bull. Mountain Man. The image of an enormous set of horns and over a ton of muscle and mean sprang to mind. He broke into a lope, meeting her halfway. "Is he all right? Where is he?"

"His leg. He needs the doctor, but he is so stubborn."

Jake was through the back door and into the kitchen before she could say anything more. His mentor and friend sprawled on a kitchen chair, his head on the table, and one badly swollen leg stretched out in front of him. His jeans were ripped and dirty. Sweat dampened his plaid shirt. His winter-gray Resistol lay discarded on the table next to his elbow.

"Manny, let's get you to the E.R. Let the doc check this out." Jake went to his knee next to the injured leg.

Manny raised his head. Sweat beaded his face. "*No es nada.* It's nothing."

"Better get that boot off while we can. You're looking pale, friend."

A hint of the Mexican's humor glinted in his eyes. "No one ever said that about me before."

Jake reached for the heel of Manny's boot. "This is coming off before your leg swells too much. Brace yourself. It's gonna hurt."

Paulina put her capable hands on the lower leg while Manny gripped his knee. "He is a stubborn man. That bull is no good for nothing."

The foot had already begun to swell but Jake carefully slipped off the boot. "Mountain Man got you good. You're lucky not to be in worse shape."

Manny didn't reply. He sat with shoulders hunched, holding his knee with both hands.

Pauline moved to his side and placed shaky fingers on her husband's shoulder. "You scare me this time, Immanuel. I could not close the chute fast enough."

Manny patted her hand. "Not your fault. The latch sticks."

"I'll pull my truck up to the back door." Jake stood. "Think you can hobble along with one of us on each side?"

Manny, jaw tight with pain, nodded. "I will try. The other leg is not so good either. The bull, he stepped on my ankle. I am not so fast anymore."

"We'll figure it out, but you're going to the E.R., either in my truck or an ambulance."

"I will get in the truck. No ambulance."

After a few harried tries and more groans than Jake had ever heard come from his old friend, Manny was loaded in the bed of the pickup along with a pillow and a quilt. The cab rose too high, so a windy ride in the back with Paulina at his side was the best they could do.

Driving more carefully than he had the day of his driver's

exam, Jake grimaced over every bump and rut on the way to Gabriel's Crossing Hospital. Upon arrival, the medical team assisted Manny into a wheelchair and wheeled him inside the hometown facility.

Small and staffed by familiar locals, the hospital lacked the equipment of larger towns but did its best to serve the community with compassionate care. He'd learned of their kindness the hard way when he'd driven Quinn, bleeding and shocky, to the E.R. that long ago November day.

He swallowed down the memory and focused on the inside of the hospital. It hadn't changed much. Now, as then, shiny silver tinsel and multicolored lights swooped around the walls, a cheery contrast to a serious place. No one came here to celebrate Christmas.

Paulina hurried alongside her husband, hands fluttering in distress, speaking in rapid-fire Spanish as she often did when excited. Manny's voice, though pained, softly reassured his wife.

In rodeo, getting injured was a given. Jake had assisted lots of buddies out of the arena, into the locker rooms and even to emergency rooms. He was no stranger to the smells and activities involved in patching up a man in conflict with a bull. But this was Manny.

He plopped in a waiting room chair and checked out the magazines. *Country Hunter* caught his eye. A deer hunter in a camo jacket displayed his prize buck. Jake covered the reminder with an issue of *People* and turned his attention to the television in one corner. Opposite him, a woman sat beside a teenage boy in a boot cast. The boy's football jersey identified him as a Gabriel's Crossing player.

"Football injury," the woman said when she saw the direction of Jake's gaze.

This was not a conversation he wanted to have. "Bad deal."

"Yeah," The kid grinned. "But we won, and I made the tackle."

"Congratulations."

An hour passed before Manny reappeared. In the meantime, Jake listened to the boy tell of football exploits, checked his text messages and phoned his grandmother who, Flo claimed, was going to Mexico in January on her own two feet.

January. Precisely when foreclosure loomed. He understood. She wanted to escape from the terrible humiliation of losing her home. He wanted her to go. He owed her everything and had failed her completely. Somehow he would send her on that cruise, and he would stay here and fight for the house.

His stomach growled. He checked the time, saw he'd missed lunch and went to the vending machine for a bag of peanuts. A blue-clad orderly pushing an empty gurney clattered off the single elevator.

Jake hoped the stretcher wasn't for Manny. Pocketing the peanuts, he sat down again, propped his elbows on his knees and with clasped hands to his forehead, prayed that Manny's injuries weren't serious enough for surgery and for a quick recovery.

He thought about phoning Allison. She'd want to know about Manny's accident. After a few starts and stops, he decided against it. If he was stuck in Gabriel's Crossing, he'd need self-control. He couldn't call her or see her every time he wanted to. He had to learn to keep a distance, to steer clear of the Buchanons in order to keep the peace.

A hand touched his back seconds before the scent of honeysuckle wove into this consciousness. His heart gave one hard thud. Allison. Even in a dark room, he could recognize her presence. So much for keeping the peace.

"Hey," he said, looking up, painfully grateful for her presence.

"How's Manny?" She took the chair next to him.

He shifted toward her. In a red skirt and white, button-down sweater, she looked fresh and young, like the cheerleader she'd once been. "No word."

"Was he hurt bad?"

"Hard to tell. I don't think so, but he's in X-ray. I'm waiting for someone to tell me. What are you doing here?"

"Paulina called. I was on lunch break anyway." She shrugged. "She said you were here."

Which meant she'd come to support him and his friends. He shouldn't be glad, but he was. "Thanks."

"I could get us something to eat."

He lifted the pack of peanuts. "I'll share."

"Not enough. I want a sandwich." She started to the vending machine as a heavy door opened and a wheelchair bearing Manny rolled through. Both legs stuck straight out, a wrap on his ankle and a hard brace on his knee with ice packs on both.

Jake stood. "You look like a trussed turkey."

Manny laughed, but his eyes were glassy. "It is not so bad."

"So he says on pain medicine." Paulina smacked her lips in a tsking sound.

"I will be on my feet soon."

The nurse stepped away from the wheelchair. "Let me get your orders from the doctors and you'll be ready to go."

"What does the doc say?" Jake asked after the nurse left.

"Ligaments and muscles. Nothing too bad." This from Manny.

"No broken bones but his ankle and leg are not good for walking. If he takes care, no surgery. If not—" Paulina stiffened her posture. "He must stay off his feet for a few weeks, and I will see that he does."

Jake knew prolonged inactivity wouldn't set well with the busy rancher. He had cattle to care for, rodeos to attend. An outdoor man chafed at being stuck inside.

He thought of the job he'd planned to ask for, but now such a request seemed cold and callous. A friend helped a friend when he was down, the way Manny always had. He didn't expect pay.

"Crutches," Manny said. "The doc says I can use crutches."

"After a week when the ankle is better, you can use crutches. For now, you will hire that Winton boy to care for the animals." Paulina crossed her arms in a gesture that clearly indicated there was to be no argument.

"No need to hire anyone," Jake said. "I'll take care of the ranch until you're able."

"I cannot ask you to do this," Manny said.

"You didn't. I offered. I'm not doing anything but rusting and getting on Granny Pat's nerves."

Manny's head tilted back in a relieved sigh. "You are God sent, my friend."

He was nothing of the kind. Time at the ranch would keep him busy, away from the Buchanons and trouble. He cut a glance toward the pretty brunette. Away from Allison, too.

"We have bulls to haul on Saturday. Tim is good help but too young and inexperienced for this." Manny's face pinched in worry. He had a scrape near his ear, evidence that the bull had gotten closer than any of them wanted to think about. "I do not want a reputation as a stock contractor who does not show up."

Paulina put a hand on his shoulder. "They will understand."

But Jake knew how small rodeos worked. If Morales bulls had been advertised, riders would enter for that opportunity alone. Replacing advertised bulls was bad for business.

"Where?"

"Durant, a one night Bullnanza."

"I'll take them."

Manny perked up. "You will?"

"No problem at all." A full day away from Gabriel's Crossing? He jumped at the chance. "I'll ask Flo to stay over with Granny Pat."

Paulina clasped her hands to her chest. "*Gloria a Dios. Gracias,* Jake."

Jake hooked an arm around Paulina's shoulders. She was still shaking. The couple had no children, and Manny was her world.

"Will you cook tamales when I get back?" he teased, hoping to ease her stress.

She patted his chest. "I have tamal in the freezer now. Come. Take us home." Suddenly all business and in her element, she motioned to Allison. "You come, too. I make plenty."

Allison shook her head. "Sounds so good, but I have to get back to work. Rain check?"

"Always you are welcome at my table."

"I'm glad you'll be okay, Manny." Allison hitched her tiny purse onto one shoulder.

"Gracias for coming."

To Jake she said, "What time Saturday morning?"

He tilted his head. "What?"

"To the rodeo. What time are you leaving?"

"Early. Probably six?" He shot a questioning glance toward Manny who nodded.

"Great," she said. "I'll see you then."

She was out the door before he comprehended her meaning. He started to follow her. "No, wait, Allison."

Paulina stopped him with a hand on his arm. "Save your breath, Jake. That one has a mind of her own. She will go." Paulina's hand patted him. "And you will be glad."

Chapter Ten

Allison disliked deceit, especially when she was the guilty party. She considered herself an honest person, but she was not about to tell anyone in her family that she was headed to Durant with a load of bulls and Jake Hamilton. Not after their behavior at the wedding. For once, the brothers four were not going to get in her way.

Jake, on the other hand, might.

She arrived at the Double M Ranch at five forty-five while the moon still hung flat and white against a bruised marble sky. Beneath a floodlight, a large stock trailer was parked outside the huge silver barn. Bulls moved against the metal insides in a series of thuds and clangs, their bovine scent strong in the chilled morning air.

Allison hugged herself against the cold and walked toward the truck. A gate clanged and Jake came around the side of the trailer. Her heart lurched.

"Hey, cowboy." She kept her voice low in case the Moraleses still slept.

Jake spun toward her on his boots, his hat shadowing his face. He didn't say anything for a second or two and when he finally spoke, the words were more resigned than welcoming. "You came."

"Happy Saturday to you, too." Was he disappointed? Mad? Had she pushed too hard? A sudden, uncharacteristic insecurity gripped her. "I won't go if you don't want me to."

Without answering, he reached inside the cab of the truck and took out a jacket. The dome light illuminated the sculpted angles of his face. Solemn. Serious.

She walked up to him, stuck her palms in her back jeans' pockets, jittery, unsure, and a little afraid she'd finally made the ultimate fool of herself. "Jake?"

"Did you tell them?"

"Who?" But she knew what he was asking.

"Don't play dumb. You snuck off, didn't you?"

"I don't have to tell anyone where I go."

"That's what I figured."

"Jake, stop. This is me and you, not my family."

His shoulders heaved once in a heavy sigh. He looked toward the purple sky and then down at her. "You don't know when to give up, do you?"

Not when it comes to you. Her confidence flagged lower. Since his return, Jake had kept her at arm's length, she thought because of her brothers. But were they really the reason? Did he simply not want her around?

She'd believed he needed forgiveness and healing and a second chance. She'd believed he'd walked away from their budding romance to protect her. Now she wondered. Had he been trying to let her down easy, and she was too dumb to know it?

"Are you trying to run me off?"

"Would it do any good?"

"Only if you meant it."

A soft huff escaped his lips. He removed his hat, studied the lining and slapped the Stetson back in place. "Get in the truck. I brought coffee and Ding Dongs for the road."

"You brought Ding Dongs?" A grin started inside her

and spread all over her body. He'd brought her favorite morning junk food.

"Don't let a box of Ding Dongs go to your head. I eat, too."

Allison threw her arms around him in a quick hug. "You scared me for a minute. I thought you didn't want me to go with you."

"I don't."

Confused, she stepped away, but he caught her and reeled her in for a genuine hug—arms around each other, bodies close, the denim of his jacket pleasantly rough against her cheek. Allison's mood went from uncertain to happy faster than a bull could bawl.

"Stop worrying," she murmured to his chest.

"Easy for you to say." He tugged the back of her hair and stepped away. "Hop in, trouble. We're on our way."

The trip took a little more than an hour and by the time they reached the rodeo grounds in Durant, the sun shone bright in the east and Allison had succeeded in prying conversation from her companion. Talk between them was easy once the words started flowing. They could talk about anything—except the terrible accident that still affected their lives. For that, there seemed no resolution, though Allison prayed every night that God would show her a way to break the impasse.

After settling the bulls at the rodeo grounds, they roamed around Durant and found a café for a real breakfast. The bacon-scented restaurant housed a mix of college students and cowboys, some of whom Jake knew. Allison wasn't surprised that he was well liked. Her brothers didn't know what they were missing.

After fueling up on eggs and bacon, they spent most of the day either checking on the bulls who didn't seem to need them at all or talking to other rodeo people. Jake put her on some guy's horse and teased when her short legs wouldn't reach the stirrups. She rode around in a circle anyway, grateful that the horse knew more than she did.

Later, they strolled through the vendors' exhibits, tried on braided belts, admired beautifully tooled leather goods and Western Christmas ornaments and gifts. Allison considered a pair of dangly silver earrings while Jake donned a dozen different cowboy hats. When they walked with fingers laced, they pretended the connection was necessary to keep from getting separated in the growing crowd.

When the rodeo began, a woman with long flowing hair in a glittery shirt and hat rode out into the arena on a paint horse, the American flag held high. With the lights dimmed and the anthem playing, she loped round and round the dirt-covered venue in a throat-filling display of patriotism.

Allison sat with Jake on a hard wooden bleacher next to the bull pen. The bulls, docile now, milled quietly around, waiting for their chances in the spotlight.

"Want some cotton candy?" he asked.

"More junk food?"

"You don't want cotton candy?"

She grinned. "Well, yeah. Of course I do."

As they strolled to the concession, Allison saw the admiring glances Jake garnered as they passed groups of women. Naturally, women noticed him with his lean good looks and cowboy swagger. Jake seemed oblivious, and Allison felt ridiculously glad about that.

"Those girls are ogling you." She nudged him with her elbow.

"Yeah?" He ripped off a piece of blue spun sugar and stuck it to her lips. "They're like you, after my cotton candy."

She licked the sticky sweetness from her lips and reached for another bite. "*My* cotton candy."

"See what I mean?"

She poked a wad of spun sugar in his open mouth and grinned. "I'm glad I made you bring me along."

"Me, too."

Deep down, she'd known that, but hearing him say the words was a new high.

The bull riding event started with a whimper, and halfway through, Manny's bulls were ahead of the riders.

"Does Manny get paid more if the cowboys fall off?"

Jake nodded. "That's the plan."

"Can you ride that one?" she asked when Manhandler dumped a cowboy in the dirt.

"Haven't ever drawn him, but maybe. He has a pattern. Out of the chute to the right for two or three bucks before he goes into a spin in the other direction. It's that misdirection that gets cowboys off balance."

"You are so smart."

He laughed, tugged her hair. "You're cute."

Allison didn't mind being cute, but she wanted to be a lot more than that to Jake Hamilton.

Jake thought he'd done pretty well all day. He'd handled Manny's stock without problem and most of all, he'd enjoyed Allison's company without getting romantic. He'd worried about that, had prayed she wouldn't show up this morning, but when she had, he'd been way too happy to have her hop in his truck and go along for the ride. Yet, he'd kept a respectful distance and only held her hand. That tiny hand with the soft, smooth skin and the single mole beside the thumb.

Little Allison Buchanon had him in knots, but he knew his part and he was proud of how he'd handled the day.

A man did what a man had to do to protect the people he lo—liked.

By the time they returned to Manny's ranch, they were both worn slick as river rocks. The long day had crept into early morning with another white moon and a splash of the Milky Way across a black sky.

She hadn't told her family. That part bugged him, even though common sense dictated the less said the better.

Still, she hadn't wanted them to know.

Was she ashamed of him? He wasn't a fool. Allison cared for him, always had, in her Pollyanna way of championing the underdog, but her family was her life and livelihood. As they should be.

"Can you handle the gates?" he asked.

She flexed her biceps. "I'm small but mighty. Tell me what to do and I'm your girl."

He refused to let his mind go there. She wasn't his girl. Never would be. She belonged here in Gabriel's Crossing with a good man and a couple of kids. A really good man. A man who didn't mess up, who was liked by the family she loved more than anything.

Choking on the thought, he hopped out of the truck and headed around to the back.

Still peppy at this late hour, probably due to the extra shots of espresso they'd had en route, Allison helped him unload the bulls, opening and closing gates on command. A light came on in the Morales kitchen and Paulina appeared in the doorway, a golden glow around her black hair. Jake went to her, assured her the bulls were secure and all was well.

"How's Manny?"

"Sleeping. Pain pills knock him out." Pulling her robe tight, she asked, "I make you coffee or food?"

Jake shook his head. "Too late. Go back to bed, Paulina."

The Mexican woman tiptoed up and kissed his cheek. "You are a good boy, the son we never had."

His chest tightened with affection. He patted her back awkwardly. "Good night, Paulina. I'll be here tomorrow."

"Sleep first. The cows will wait."

"Sure."

She closed the door, and Jake turned to find Allison right behind him in the darkness. The temperature had dropped and she shivered.

"Paulina's a nice lady." Allison's lips trembled.

"You're cold." Jake removed his jacket and wrapped the fleece inside around her shoulders. He tugged the collar close beneath her chin, his hands lingering there.

Someday a worthy man would stand in his spot and shed his jacket for the sweetest girl in Gabriel's Crossing.

Jake pondered the roil of emotion that came with that inevitable fact.

Inside the house the light went out, but he could see Allison's big brown eyes in the moon's glow. He could hear the soft puffs of her breath and feel her shivers.

Penned cattle moved about, mooing softly. Their restlessness resonated in him. He was restless, too, yearning for things he couldn't have and shouldn't want.

Allison rested her hands on either side of his waist. Through his shirt, he felt the coolness of her fingers against his skin. He moved in closer, sharing his heat. His brain pulsated with the thought that some other guy would hold her.

"I should get you home," he murmured, and heard the husky roughness of his words.

"I know."

But neither of them moved. They were cocooned there

together on the Double M, and all day they'd been away from the distractions of town and family. A man's head could get muddled.

"Jake," she said on a breathy whisper.

"Yeah?" She lifted her face so the light reflected on her skin. Such a pretty, happy, caring face. He placed a palm against her cheek. "You're so soft."

He hadn't meant to say that.

She put her arms around his neck. His jacket fell away, rustled to the ground at their feet. He let it go.

He really wanted to kiss her. To hold her for a little while there in the quiet cold and absorb the essence of Allison. Before some other man took his place.

So he did. He had no right, knew he didn't, but he kissed her anyway.

Her lips were cold, her mouth warm as she sighed into him. He closed his eyes and held her face between his calloused hands, pulse thrumming in his head. A voice somewhere in the back of his brain tapped out a warning. Jake didn't listen. He kissed her, kissed the corner of her mouth, her eyelids, her hair. And when he was done, he rested his chin on her hair and held her close.

Allison. Her name reverberated through him.

"I love you, Jake." Her voice was muffled against his shoulder so that he could almost pretend he hadn't heard. But the slam of emotion shook him to his bootheels.

She couldn't be. He wouldn't let her be in love with him.

Fighting the wild exultation and the equally wild anxiety, he shook his head and tried to back away. Tried and failed. Allison was a sticky web of sugar holding him captive.

"Are you crazy?" His voice was a shaky whisper. Hadn't she admitted her brothers hated him? That she'd avoided telling her family about the rodeo because of him? And hadn't he reconciled to the idea that she'd find a better man?

"You took my heart when you left Gabriel's Crossing years ago." Her voice was soft and sweet with a tinge of hurt that set his soul aching. "I never got it back."

"We were kids." Jake kept his tone even, though his fingers touched her face and stroked her velvet cheek while he wished he was half the man she thought he was. "Too young to fall in love."

"We're not kids now."

"Ah, Allison." He shook his head, fighting emotion. Allison sucked his breath away, stole his last brain cell and filled him with such foolish hope. He pulled her in close and stared down into the most honest brown eyes possible. "We can't do this."

"Why?"

"You know why. Your family had a fit over a simple dance at a wedding. You didn't even tell them about today. That's meaningful." She opened her mouth to deny it, but he stopped her with a finger to her soft, moist lips. "Don't say it isn't. No amount of optimism will make the Buchanons accept me, and you're a Buchanon to the bone."

"We'll find a way. Give us a chance, Jake."

There was no chance for them. He'd known nine years ago. He knew now.

"I'll be helping Manny for a while and taking care of some other business, but I won't stay in this town forever. I won't do that to myself or your brother." *Or you.*

He didn't say the rest, the one thing he longed for but couldn't have. He'd never ask her to choose him over her family, because that's exactly what she'd have to do. And separation from family would break her heart more than his leaving ever could. She belonged with the Buchanons here in Gabriel's Crossing, not ostracized with a rodeo cowboy. Love between the pair of them was out of the question, no matter how much he cared for her.

She stared at him for a long, painful moment while he heard the earth crack around him. Or maybe that was his heart. Then, she bent to retrieve his jacket, holding out the now-chilled denim. "You shouldn't go around kissing a girl if you don't mean it."

She turned away and started toward her car.

He'd hurt her anyway—the last thing he'd intended, the reason he'd planned never to kiss her. He caught her elbow. She kept walking, and his boot toe stumped in the dirt in his haste to keep up with her.

"I do mean it. I did." Frustration laced his words. How did he fix this without saying too much? "You're special, Allison."

She stopped. "Am I? Really?"

She looked so vulnerable and those honest brown eyes were wounded.

"You know you are." He wouldn't kiss her again. He wouldn't even hold her. Nothing good could come of either.

She walked into his chest and laid her head on his heart. He tried not to put his arms around her but couldn't bear the thought that he'd hurt her more if he refused.

"I love you, Jake," she whispered again. And he bit his tongue to keep from saying the words back to her.

Chapter Eleven

Jake didn't like to miss church but he didn't want to see Allison. Not this morning. Not after he'd wrestled and prayed and tried to make sense of his life all through what was left of the night. She loved him. He'd known that, had probably known it for years, though he'd refused to let the information seep into his thick head.

What did a man do about a woman he couldn't have who loved him anyway?

He had no answer and apparently this morning, God wasn't sharing.

While he fretted, he phoned Manny, drank enough coffee to recharge a car battery and cooked flapjacks for himself and Granny Pat. When he offered to drive his grandmother to church, she refused, claiming they played the music too loud and gave her a headache. She always said that, but then, no one in his family had ever cared much for church. He was still amazed at the change in his own life even though he wondered why God had sent him back into the mess in Gabriel's Crossing.

After Granny Pat settled in the recliner with the morning newspaper, Jake took his cowboy Bible and another cup of high-octane coffee out on the back porch.

He was glad for the excuse to escape to Manny's ranch this afternoon when Florence arrived. She was threatening to drag out Christmas decorations and send him on top of the house, but he wasn't in the mood.

He opened to a random page in Matthew and read:

You have heard that it was said, "You shall love your neighbor and hate your enemy." But I say to you, Love your enemies and pray for those who perse- cute you, so that you may be sons of your Father who is in heaven. For he makes his sun rise on the evil and on the good, and sends rain on the just and on the unjust. For if you love those who love you, what reward do you have?

With leaves blowing around his feet and the sun hid- ing behind a flat gray sky, he pondered the verses. What was Jesus saying? That he shouldn't love Allison if she loved him? Or that he should love her brothers regardless of their anger?

His cell phone vibrated against his hip. Expecting Manny or Paulina, he didn't bother to read caller ID.

"Hello."

"Hamilton, I think you know what this call is about."

"Who is this?" He held the phone out so he could read the display and didn't recognize the number.

"Brady Buchanon. I figured you'd be expecting my call."

Jake's mind raced through the possibilities and the only thing he could come up with was Allison and their trip to the rodeo. He didn't want her taking the brunt of Brady's animosity. Not because of him.

"What I do is none of your business."

"Trashing another Buchanon construction project *is* my business."

Jake's brain did a quick recalculate. So this wasn't about

yesterday's rodeo? He didn't know whether to be relieved or shaken. "I don't know what you're talking about."

"Right." Brady's voice was thick with sarcasm. "We have an unfriendly little chitchat at Faith's wedding and then suddenly when the guys are off work yesterday and no one is around, a second job site is trashed. This time the Bartowski house. You trying to tell me that's *another* coincidence?"

Yesterday, while he was with Allison at the rodeo an hour away, something Brady appeared not to know. And Jake wasn't about to tell him. Allison had made her intentions clear. She claimed to love him, but she didn't want to get grief from her family. And who could blame her? He couldn't do much for her but he could do this.

"Can't help you, Brady."

"You're done messing with the Buchanons, cowboy. The first time might have been coincidence but not two in a row. I'm pressing charges this time." The line went dead.

So much for loving his enemies. They didn't seem too eager to receive.

With his stomach rolling, Jake stared at the cell phone. He wasn't worried about the law. Witnesses knew where he'd been. Allison knew. He realized then that she'd hear about the vandalism and jump right in the middle of the storm unless he told her to stay out of harm's way.

He punched in her number but the call went straight to voice mail. This was his problem and he'd handle it. Even if he had to confess to something he hadn't done.

He stuck his head inside the house and yelled, "I'll be back in a while, Granny Pat. Call if you need me."

Leaving his Bible and coffee cup on the lawn chair, he headed across town to the Buchanon Construction site.

The place was crawling with Buchanons. Every last one of the males and a couple of what he figured were contractors. Big burly guys in tool belts with clipboards and angry expressions. Nobody liked being called out on Sunday, especially for a problem of this nature.

He did a quick scan of the property to see what he was supposed to have done. Red spray paint covered the brick outside in graffiti. A couple of windows were busted out. Glass sparkled on the red dirt.

Jake's stomach soured. He wondered how bad the inside was.

Bad enough to skip church. Bad enough to call the cops.

A Gabriel's Crossing patrol car was parked next to the Buchanon trucks, and a uniformed officer he didn't recognize snapped photos of the damage. Nerves jumping, Jake crossed the unfinished yard and headed toward Dan Buchanon. The family father looked like an impending thunderstorm, a supercell about to spawn a F5 tornado.

One of the men saw Jake and said something to the Buchanon patriarch. Conversation stopped as all eyes turned on the accused.

"What are you doing here?" As tall as his sons and graying at the temples of his black hair, Dan wore a Buchanon Construction ball cap and a scowl aimed directly at Jake.

"Had a call from Brady." Jake stopped in front of the older man, never his favorite Buchanon, and chose his words carefully. "He seems to think I had something to do with his."

Before Dan could speak, Quinn appeared from inside the damaged house, eyes narrowed, face grim. "Where were you yesterday, Jake? Specifically last night?"

Though Jake struggled not to react to his former best friend, a tight fist clenched in his chest. "Durant. At a rodeo."

"You better have witnesses to prove that."

"I do."

"Don't be naive, Quinn." Brady's scowl was dark and threatening. "No one worked this site yesterday, and. Durant's not that far away. He could have hit the house before or after his rodeo and used the trip as an alibi."

"I didn't. I left early yesterday morning and returned early this morning."

A car door slammed. In his peripheral vision Jake saw Allison, in her Sunday dress, zooming across the dirt yard like a bumblebee. He whirled toward her and pointed. "Go home."

Her footsteps slowed. "What's going on?"

Jake's blood pressure ratcheted up a few notches. The last person he wanted in the middle of this mess was Allison. "Nothing that concerns you. Go home. Stay out of it."

But Allison, as Paulina had said, had a mind of her own. Brown eyes wide and concerned, she marched up to Quinn. "Jayla got a text that said someone vandalized another job site."

"Yeah, and cowboy here claims he was at rodeo all day," Brady said. "Isn't that convenient?"

"He was."

Jake's heart tumbled lower than a snake's belly.

Sawyer turned blue eyes on his sister. "How would you know?"

"Go home, Allison." Why couldn't she stay out of this? Jake took her elbow and glared down at her, telegraphing the message. *Keep quiet.* "Go. Now. You're not wanted here. Let me handle this."

"Let you handle it? So you can take the blame for something you didn't do? Just to keep my name out of it?" She gave her arm a jerk and pulled away. "I'm not afraid of my family, Jake. I don't need your protection."

But there was a time she had and the memory flashed between them like lightning. He had to get her out of here fast.

"Let me do this, Allison."

"You were going to lie for me, weren't you? You would have confessed to a crime because of me. Wouldn't you?"

Yeah, he would have. "Why can't you leave well enough alone?"

Five hulking men glared at Jake. "What is she talking about?"

Allison swung toward her brothers.

"I'll tell you what *she's* talking about." Allison slammed a doubled fist against her blue sweater. "*She* went to the rodeo with Jake yesterday. All day. From before dawn until early this morning. I was with Jake every single minute. He did not vandalize this property."

Her words rang on the Sunday-morning air like the ring of a hammer on steel. The Buchanons went from thunderstruck to thunderheads. Jake simply stared up into the sky and shook his head. His good intentions withered in the morning sun. She melted him, disarmed him.

"You agreed to stay clear of him, Allison." Quinn's voice was a Rottweiler growl.

"No, Quinn, you said that I should. I never *agreed* to anything. And I won't."

Quinn's glare burned into his sister with a mix of disbelief and anger. "You'd betray your own flesh and blood for a lying rodeo bum?"

"Whoa, hey, hold up." The usually quiet Dawson stepped between Jake and his brothers, his red fleece jacket like a stoplight. "If Allison says they were together, this conversation is over."

"The very fact that they were together for close to twenty-four hours says it's not."

"Come on, Brady, be reasonable." Dawson turned up both palms, persuading. "The man was willing to take on all five of us to protect our sister. He was willing to take responsibility to keep us off her back. That means something in my book."

"What it means to me is deception. Which proves how bad he is for her. He convinced her to sneak off with him—secretly."

Dawson shook his head. "Not the way I see the situation."

Quinn's left hand kneaded his right bicep as if the damaged arm pained him, an absent gesture that struck Jake to the bone. He'd caused all of this. The damage to Quinn and now problems for Allison.

Allison made a disgusted sound. "This is a ridiculous conversation. Jake didn't make me do anything and that includes sneaking off. My idea. My choice. Tell them, Jake. You didn't even want me to go."

Jake pushed back the sides of his jean jacket and fisted his hands on his hips. He wasn't going to make her look like the villain. "I've got one thing to say and then I'm out of here. I'm not responsible for your construction problems, Brady, and I'm tired of your finger-pointing, but you're right about one thing. Family matters more than anything. I learned that the hard way."

While the Buchanon clan absorbed his words, Jake spun on his boots and headed for the ranch.

Allison spent the afternoon at her apartment, opting not to attend the weekly family dinner and football game. She pulled out her tiny Christmas tree but didn't have the energy to put it up. She made a Skype call to Faith who was still in St. Thomas and from the joy on her friend's newly tanned face and the constant references to Derrick, Faith was one happy bride. In true best friend form, Allison didn't mention her problems with Jake and her brothers, though she wished she could talk to someone who would understand.

The problem was she didn't really understand herself. She was quite positive Jake loved her, but in his twisted viewpoint, love wasn't enough. To her, love was everything. But she loved her family, too, and loathed feeling like the odd man out.

She'd been too aggravated to go to Mom's today. Aggravated and unwilling to face the harassment about Jake and the ridiculous accusation. Again. Couldn't they understand that Jake Hamilton was a good, responsible man doing his best not to hurt anyone?

In her comfy gray sweats and fuzzy socks, she made a cup of cocoa topped with fat marshmallows and turned on the football game. She really should get a dog like Brady's, or a cat. Watching alone wasn't the same as watching with the rowdy Buchanons.

She blew on her hot chocolate. Was this the way things would be if she chose Jake over family? Would they really throw her out of the clan? Or would they include her in family gatherings but ignore the man she loved? Either option broke her heart but so did the thought of a future without Jake.

She wanted the man and she wanted her family. She wanted a happy ever after like Faith had found.

Settling in a tan easy chair—one of Mom's discards— she curled her legs beneath her and cradled the warm cocoa in her hands. The Cowboys were down twenty-one to seven, the offense struggling to move the ball. The brothers would be going crazy about now, yelling at the quarterback and formulating better plays while munching hot links or shoveling Fritos into Dad's ever-popular Ro*Tel dip.

She wondered what new green recipe Jayla had brought this week. And if Quinn was guzzling Red Diamond tea out of nervous energy. Brady and Dawg were probably sprawled like rugs on the floor, taking up way too much space. Dawg's big old tail would thump like mad when the Buchanons celebrated a touchdown as if he, too, cheered their favorite team. The twins, she knew, would be wearing blue-and-silver Dallas Cowboys jerseys, one of the few look-alike items they shared these days.

She sipped the sweet cocoa. This is what life would be like without family. Lonely. Missing them.

Was this how Jake felt after the accident? Was this how he felt now?

Someone knocked on the door and her heart leaped, hoping her visitor was Jake. It wasn't.

A gorgeous man in a Dallas Cowboys jersey stood on her square concrete porch. "Dawson."

He held up a bag of Fritos and a plastic container. "Delivery service. Chip and dip."

"I was hoping for barbecue weenies."

"In that case—" He pivoted as if to leave.

She snagged his jersey sleeve. "On second thought, chip and dip sounds great. Is that Dad's famous Ro*Tel?"

"Yep. Spicy hot. Guaranteed to take the hair off your tongue."

"The Cowboys are losing."

"Don't remind me." He set the foods on the coffee table, a chunky rectangle of distressed wood she'd bought at an estate sale. Brady and Sawyer had refinished the piece into a thing of beauty.

"Why aren't you at Mom's?"

"I missed my little sister. You seemed glum this morning after the—" he shrugged "—you know. Thought you might need a friend." His blue eyes were full of sympathy. "I could ask you the same thing. Why aren't you with the fam?"

"I wasn't up to it today."

"Jake?"

"I don't want to fight with them—or you—about him."

"Not why I'm here." Her brother ripped open the Fritos and offered her the bag. "This morning at the site, I saw something in Hamilton that got me thinking."

She took out a handful of chips but didn't eat; the salty corn smell lifted to her nose "Why do things have to be this way, Dawson? Why can't the family forgive and move on?"

"That's what I was thinking about. Prayed about it a little, too. We seem to be stuck back there nine years ago." He dipped his chip and crunched, chewing while he gazed at the television in a distracted manner. "Remember how things were before the shooting? Quinn's football picture was on posters in all the store windows. His name was in every Saturday morning coffee shop conversation."

Allison smiled, nostalgic. "I can almost hear Red Chambers reliving the play-by-play down at Darla's Doughnuts. *'Quinn back to pass. He scrambles, dodges a tackler. Then two. No one's open. But like a surgeon he slices through the defense and finds a receiver in double coverage. Twenty-five yard pass. No one could make more out of nothing than Quinn Buchanon.'*"

"He was grand marshal in every parade. Doted on by everyone in town. Recruiters, too. The rest of us should have been jealous, but I was so proud to call him brother. I idolized him."

"We all did, Dawson. The whole town did."

"He was going to put Gabriel's Crossing on the map. Heck, he was already doing it. News media followed him around like a rock star. *Sports Illustrated* did an article, comparing him to greats like Joe Montana." Dawson sighed, the chip in his hand forgotten. "Then the shooting happened and everything changed. We changed. Quinn changed. The town grieved, too."

"And someone had to take the blame."

"Yeah. We needed a scapegoat to focus our anger on. Human nature is an interesting thing." He grinned a little. "Psych 101 keeps coming back to haunt me."

Allison picked at the Fritos, remembering those terrible, painful days. "Human nature or whatever, Jake hurt, too. But no one cared about one stray kid who wasn't that great at football."

"No one but you." He popped the chip in his mouth, his blue, blue eyes on her.

"He needed someone." And she needed him. He knew her secret but never judged her, never spoke of it. Instead, he made her feel safe again.

Not that she could share any of that with Dawson.

She dipped into Dad's cheesy concoction and watched it drip into the container.

"You had a crush on him."

She hiked a shoulder, conceding the truth. No point in arguing. "I was trying to do the right thing."

"You infuriated the family. Even Mom and Dad were upset about the amount of time you spent with Jake."

"I didn't think they knew." Just as they hadn't known how badly she'd needed his friendship."

"They knew. We all did. Gabriel's Crossing is a small town and anything a Buchanon does is news."

Not everything.

"Or fodder for the grapevine." She reached for the remote and muted the television. The Cowboys, like her, were struggling.

"You have to remember, sis, it was a terrible year. Everyone was hurting, especially Quinn. Surgeries, rehab and the painful knowledge that he would never throw another touchdown pass. He had some bad juju going on. Still does."

"Are you saying Mom and Dad had their hands full without me consorting with the enemy?"

"I guess you could put it that way."

"Is that why you boys threatened him?"

Dawson tilted back into the nubby couch cushions. "Did he tell you that? Because it's a lie."

"No, he's said nothing negative about any of you. Jake isn't mad. He's full of regret."

Dawson pondered her words over a few more dipped Fritos that had him clutching his throat. "I gotta have something to drink. Dad went heavy on the jalapeños today."

"There's pop in the fridge. I'll get you one." She jumped up, returning with a cold can of Coke.

Dawson popped the tab and took a long pull. He swallowed and emitted a long sigh. "Ah, better. Man, that stuff's hot."

"You're a good brother, Dawson."

"I'm not taking sides."

No, he wouldn't. Buchanons didn't take sides with anyone but a Buchanon. No one but traitor Allison. "Do you think things will ever change?"

"Hard to say. Maybe. Maybe not." He set the can on the coffee table with a soft clunk.

"I love him, Dawson."

Her brother drew in a deep breath, puffed out his cheeks, and exhaled slowly. "Not the best news I've ever had, but I figured as much. You don't exactly hide your feelings well. What are you going to do?"

"I don't know. Nothing, I suppose. Jake thinks the situation is hopeless. I guess he's right." Hurting at the thought, she rubbed her forehead with her fingertips. "He'll be leaving as soon as his grandma and Manny Morales are well enough. Even if he didn't have rodeos to attend, why would he want to stay here?"

No matter how much she yearned to be the reason, she wasn't enough to hold him in the place that had hurt him so badly.

Dawson was silent, his elbows on his knees and hands clasped under his chin, he turned his eyes on the football game. He was, no doubt, thinking, worrying, brooding over the bombshell she'd exploded.

She clicked the mute button and sound returned bringing the roar of a Dallas crowd at a field goal. Three points wasn't much, but "Da Boys" were making progress.

She observed her brother, the quiet one with the tender heart and the beautiful face. All her brothers were beautiful in a rugged manly way, but Dawson and Sawyer happened to be movie star quality. Not that either of them knew it. They thought of themselves as ordinary guys, Buchanons, and loyal as sunshine. She loved them so much. All of them, no matter their faults.

"Want a sandwich?" she asked, breaking the silence.

"I'm good." He patted his belly. "Too much cheese dip."

Outside car doors slammed. The siblings exchanged glances.

"Expecting anyone?"

"No." She went to the window and peeked out. "Oh, my goodness."

"Who is it?" Dawson rose and came to join her, standing a foot taller. As she opened the door and pointed, he laughed.

A gaggle of Buchanons piled out of trucks and trailed toward her small duplex like worker ants. Dawg leaped from the back of Brady's truck and ambled toward her with his usual tongue-lolling happy face and windshield-wiper tail.

"What are you all doing?" she asked.

Her mother stopped in the doorway for a hug. "We missed you."

Except for Brady, the rest of the family flowed into her tiny space and collapsed in front of her small TV. The biggest brother picked her up, his favorite way to annoy her, and with a wicked grin said, "You jinxed the ball game."

She giggled. Playful superstitions were as much a part of the Buchanon tradition as Sunday football games. The twins always wore their favorite jerseys. Brady wore his cap. Quinn ate exactly three pancakes before a big game and then there were the barbecued weenies and dips. It was the Buchanon way. "You're blaming me because the Cowboys are losing?"

He winced. "Don't say losing. Now that we're all together, there's still time to rectify this gross injustice to our favorite team."

"The Cowboy franchise will be forever thankful to know we Buchanons hold the key to their team's winloss record."

"Got that right." Brady set her on her feet with a pat on the head. "Buchanons stick together. It makes things simpler."

She got the message. They were here. They forgave her. But Jake was still the odd man out.

Some of the pleasure in their appearance seeped out as Brady turned and picked his way over the bodies strewn about in her living room.

"Touchdown, Dallas!" Sawyer shot up from the floor in a victory dance and stepped on Jayla's leg. Jayla yelped. Dawg howled. And the rest of the family laughed.

"Did you see that?" Brady pumped his arm. "Did you see that interception? Linebacker, baby."

Allison stood in the doorway, watching the wild, crazy, wonderful Buchanons with a sad smile. Faults and all, this was family. She loved them desperately, but as she listened to their conversation and watched their antics, she made a painful decision.

They were never going to back down, never going to change. The only person who could change was her.

Family mattered, but love was everything.

Chapter Twelve

Jake had meant to stay away but somehow his truck ended up outside Allison's apartment Sunday evening after a busy afternoon at Manny's. His friend was mending, stir-crazy and eager to be at work.

Through eyes gritty with the need for sleep, Jake saw the amber glow of light inside the duplex. He also saw the Camaro in the driveway next to a Buchanon truck. He shouldn't knock. He should go back home and forget this powerful need to be with her.

He parked at the curb and sat in the truck like a crazed stalker. Head tilted back, he talked to Jesus, who seemed to reside somewhere above the gray headliner. He'd never intended to love Allison Buchanon, never wanted to, but he finally had to recognize the secret he'd been hiding in his soul for too long. She was the reason he'd never married, the reason he'd tried and failed at the engagement in Wyoming. Like Allison, he'd given his heart away a long time ago. But he hadn't been as wise as little Allison. He hadn't known.

A soft melody of love came through the CD player, country music, the tunes of lonely cowboys everywhere.

He should go. He'd call her later.

His cell phone buzzed in his pocket. One look and he laughed. From Allison.

What are you doing out there? Casing the joint? You're not stealing my plastic Cowboys mug. I know you covet it.

He texted back, Spoilsport. I really wanted that cup. Heading home now. Good night.

Before he could return the cell to his pocket and start the truck, her front door opened and there she was. Hair dancing, she charged across the lawn and yanked open the driver's side door.

"Going somewhere?"

"Didn't you get my text?"

"I got it. Didn't like it. Come on in. I made soup and need someone with a healthy appetite."

He hitched his chin toward the other vehicle. "You have company."

"Dawson's alternator went out. Brady took him home."

"You're alone?"

"Not if you're here." She tugged his sleeve. "Come on, you didn't drive across town to park on my curb and send text messages."

He grinned and got out. "Sounds silly when you put it that way."

"I'm glad you stopped by."

He didn't know if he was or not. "Did your family give you any grief?"

"No."

"You sure?"

"All's forgiven. I'm okay, Jake, but thanks for caring."

That was the crux of the matter.

"Sorry I made you mad."

She shrugged. "You were trying to protect me. Like always. But these days I can take care of myself."

Jake wasn't so sure about that.

He pushed open the front door, and the bell on the cheery red-and-green wreath tinkled.

Inside, the scent of spicy Tex-Mex seasoning filled his nose. His belly growled. "That smells great."

"I won't tell you how long I didn't slave over that."

"Huh?"

She grinned up at him, cute as ever, and his whole being was happy.

"Did you catch up on your sleep this afternoon?"

"No. Went out to Manny's."

"How is he?"

"Annoyed, but I think he likes having Paulina fuss over him all day."

"You're sweet to take care of his chores."

Sweet?

"No big deal. Manny's done a lot for me. Why was Dawson here? Problems?"

She shook her head. "The family came over to watch football."

"Nice." He followed her into the kitchen where the soup bubbled on the stove top.

"When the Cowboys lost, they all crawled out whimpering like kicked pups. Even Dawg. They wouldn't even stick around for my taco soup." She took two red ceramic bowls out of an overhead cupboard and clumped them on the counter.

"Buchanons do love their football."

"Ain't it the truth? And guess what? The twins have tickets for next week's game."

"In Dallas?"

"Cowboys Stadium." She knew the venue name had changed but to loyal fans, whereever Da Boys played would forever be Cowboy Stadium. "Nosebleed section. It'll be awesome."

"Are you jealous?"

"Green as an avocado." But her eyes twinkled with humor. "They promised to bring me a foam finger."

Jake smiled at the mental image of Allison wildly waving a blue foam finger. "Everyone's favorite."

He wanted to take her to a game. He wanted to listen to her cheerleader voice yell at the refs while he bought her overpriced hot dogs and laughed at her enthusiasm. They'd have a great time. He knew as well as he knew she'd have to fight her family to make it happen. No point in putting her in a worse situation.

So instead of offering the invitation, he took the bowl of steaming soup to the round glass table in the corner of her tiny kitchen.

"How did all the Buchanons fit inside this place?"

"Wall-to-wall bodies. The house was rocking. Brady threatened to knock out a wall but was vetoed in favor of the game."

He remembered those times of crazy chaos with the Buchanons. Remembered and missed them. "Why were they here instead of your parents' place?"

"Long story." She sliced a spoon through her soup, gathering vegetables and broth which she held in front of her mouth. Steam curled upward. She took a sip and shuddered. "Hot."

"Go figure." But he sipped, too. "Do you have any leads on who's vandalizing your properties? That's twice now. A pattern. Does someone have an ax to grind with your company?"

"I didn't ask."

"Some things are better left undiscussed?"

"Especially during a football game." She pumped her eyebrows, but he saw the truth in the worried way she glanced aside. Any conversation about the job site problems involved him, and Allison wasn't going there.

"How's your grandma today?" she asked instead.

"Feisty. She and Flo booked a cruise for January."

"No way! Will she be ready for that?"

"They think she will. She's coming along faster than I thought she would. Thanks to you and Flo. You've made her want to get stronger."

Allison put down her spoon. "Which means you'll be leaving sooner than later."

"Don't you think that's better for everyone?"

"No, I don't. And if you ask her or Manny and Paulina, I doubt they'll agree either."

She had that right. "Paulina wants to adopt me." He chuckled. "Joking, of course, but I appreciate the sentiment."

"They miss you."

"I miss them, too." *But I'll miss you, most of all.*

"Then stay, Jake. Put that one incident behind you and come home for good."

Home. He'd rambled the country for so long, home was a fantasy.

"I wish I could, but money doesn't grow on trees."

"You still haven't found a solution to the mortgage?"

He probably shouldn't have told her his concerns about the mortgage. She worried as much as he did.

"Not yet." He had enough money to live on but paying for Granny's house along with his own loan payments strained him to the max. The only solution was one he didn't want to think about yet.

She got up from the table and went to the window. She was slim as a child in her gray sweats and blue socks. Back to him, she said, "How much longer? You won't leave before January, will you?"

Jake heard the ache in her question and despised himself for putting it there. He followed her to the window, put his hands on her shoulders, massaged the fragile bones that framed the woman he loved. As much as he wanted to, he wouldn't tell her how he felt. Knowing would only hurt her more in the end, when he left.

Hurting her hurt him, though he didn't care about his own pain. He doubted she understood that either. He wasn't some melodramatic teenager anymore who thought only of himself. This was about her, about what he knew was right for Allison.

"Not sure. No longer than that."

"Not before Christmas. Please, not before Christmas."

Heaviness rode his shoulders with the weight of a Brahma bull. "I'll try."

He couldn't make promises, not with so much at stake.

Her breath made gray clouds on the windowpane. Beyond the glass, the navy blue evening pressed in, casting shadows and light through the trees. A soft mist fell, weeping softly against the pane.

"I love you," she whispered. "Doesn't that matter at all?"

He gentled his touch, stroked the sides of her slender neck. She was soft as air. He ached with wanting to tell her all that was in his heart, but knew better. What good could come of saying words that made promises he couldn't keep? Words that would only wound her deeper in the end.

In a whisper, he admitted the only thing he dared. "Yes, it matters."

He was humbled to be loved by someone as amazing as Allison Buchanon. Humbled and broken.

"I think you love me, too." Her sweet, soft voice throbbed with emotion.

"Allison." He closed his eyes, holding back the truth. The situation warred inside him. What was best for her?

What was right? Was holding back his love a kindness or a stab wound? He didn't know, so he said nothing.

"I'm starting to feel like a fool, Jake, so if you don't love me, if I'm wrong, tell me now and I won't bother you about it anymore."

He opened his mouth to do exactly that, but the words tumbled out all wrong. "I could never lie to you."

Slowly, she turned, somehow ending up in his arms, until they were heart-to-heart. "You love me, but you don't want to come between me and my family."

What could he say? "As long as I'm in this town, especially if I'm in your life, there will be trouble."

"But you do love me, don't you? Please say it, Jake. Give me that much."

Only a stronger man could look into those soft brown eyes and deny her the truth. "I love you." He tapped his left chest. "You have me heart and soul."

The joy that lit her face was as bright as Vegas rodeo lights. Her soft fingertips stroked his jawline. "Love is all we need. The rest will work out."

He wanted desperately to believe her, at least for this moment. She tiptoed up, pulled his face down and kissed him with a tenderness that made his chest throb. He returned the kiss, holding her face between his rough cowboy hands, breathing her essence.

"I love you so much," she whispered between kisses and Jake's knees trembled with the honor she bestowed on him. To be loved by such a woman was beyond anything he deserved.

Deserved. He didn't deserve her. He couldn't have her. Her family would always be a wedge that would eventually come between them.

His brain, muddled by her nearness and the great power of her love, fought for clarity. Slowly, gently, he pulled back until he could breathe again, think again. Her sweetness lingered on his lips and in his heart.

She was starry-eyed and beautiful, looking at him as if he could do anything. That's the way she made him feel. Big and strong and worthy. But he wasn't, and somehow he had to make her understand.

"Allison, listen to me. Listen."

Her smile wobbled at the seriousness of his tone. "Don't. Please Jake, don't ruin this moment."

He stepped away from temptation but couldn't bear to turn loose of her hands. That simple contact sustained him to say what must be said.

"This is crazy. No matter how we feel, love won't fix things." He shook his head against the protest he saw coming. "We can't turn back the clock and erase what I did to your brother. To your family and this town. They don't want me here. They sure don't want me to have you. As long as I'm here, they'll keep up the pressure. They'll make you miserable. I don't want you hurt."

"I can handle my family."

"You shouldn't have to. We both know as long as I'm anywhere around Gabriel's Crossing, you'll be caught in the middle. There's no solution other than my absence."

"Yes, there is." She slipped her arms around his waist and tilted her face toward his. "I'll go with you. We'll leave together."

Her sacrifice ripped through him like a bull's horn. "And say goodbye to your family? You can't do that, Allison. You wouldn't."

Soft brown eyes implored him. "Yes, I would. For you."

Because he was at a loss, he circled her with his arms and held her close. His heart in a vise, his chest exploding, he pondered what he'd done that someone as special as Allison loved him enough to give up everything that mattered.

* * *

Allison had made up her mind. When the time came, she was going away with Jake. Most of the time, she could ignore the anxious knot in her belly. The family would eventually forgive her. They'd have to. Wouldn't they?

The voice of her conscience said it was wrong. She should talk to her mother or sisters or even her pastor. But she didn't.

She had a savings account and some stock put aside. They'd be okay. She'd find another job. She'd help Jake pay off the mortgage.

Not that she'd tell him that. Not yet. His male pride would get in the way.

So with her mind made up, she prayed half-baked prayers and hurried home from work every day to see Jake. And if there was conversation about him at work, she ignored the grumbles. Brady and Quinn still believed he'd had something to do with vandalizing the property, regardless of her protests, and even though Dawson looked on her with sympathy, she'd learned to keep quiet and look forward to going home.

Today, she and Jake had escaped to the river outside of town where the muddy red waters lay like rippled stained glass and the cold front from up north had turned the grass a crisp brown and quieted the frogs and crickets. A few leaves clung for dear life to nearly naked limbs, heralding the coming winter, and a weak sun hid somewhere behind a gunmetal silver sky.

Except for waterfowl, this recreational section of the Red lay quiet and empty this late in the season, but in summer teens from Gabriel's Crossing fished and floated the calm waters on a lazy, winding five-mile stretch.

As a rule Allison preferred other places to this river, but in town privacy was impossible. She didn't like to think about that night when she'd been a foolish teenager, angry because her family refused to let her date Jake. She seldom thought about the other boy, the one Jake had slammed his fist into because of her. Or of the many tears she'd wept that night in Jake Hamilton's arms.

The past was the past. Let it stay there. Wasn't that what she always told Jake and her brothers?

Today, she and the man she loved walked along the sandy bank together, stepping over driftwood, content to be alone, holding hands while they talked about everything and nothing. The most important subject hovered like a horsefly waiting to sting. So they pretended to be a normal couple, in love, and planning for the future. Or at least Allison did. If Jake was too quiet at times, she understood. They'd never revisited her declaration, that she would leave Gabriel's Crossing when he did. She'd tried once to bring up the topic, but he'd sidestepped the issue. He was afraid for her, she knew, still insisting he would never take her away from her beloved family.

If she didn't know he loved her, she'd be hurt. But he worried about her, about how leaving her family would affect her. Allison was mature enough to know it would.

So she clung to each day they had together, praying it wouldn't be the last. Praying that when the time came, she'd have the courage to go with him, and that he would let her.

A ragged old rowboat lay on its belly on the riverbank. Jake gave the wooden structure a nudge with his boot. "Let's take a ride."

"Are you crazy?" She rubbed the chill from her upper arms and danced a little on the sand. "That old thing's been here forever. It probably leaks."

"I'm a bull rider. Crazy is my middle name." He flipped

the small craft upright and found two splintered oars beneath. "What's the worst thing that could happen?"

"We could sink!" But she was already helping him push the boat into the shallows.

"I'll save you."

Like he'd done before.

"Remember the time we were all down here fishing and you fell in?" she asked. "You flailed around like a one-legged frog."

He laughed, a free, delighted sound that warmed her bones. She loved to hear him laugh.

"How do you remember those things?"

"A woman in love remembers everything."

"When you were ten?"

She stuck out her tongue. "Well, okay, I have a great memory."

The boat splashed into the water and bobbed there. Allison held the thin, muddy tie rope while Jake searched for leaks. "Looks sound to me."

"Like you're a boat expert."

"Hey, careful, little girl. You're insulting a man who once owned a twenty-foot bass boat."

"Really?"

"What? You thought all I could do was ride bulls and horses?"

"Of course not. You're a really good kisser, too." She wrinkled her nose at him. "Do you still have a boat? We could go fishing sometime."

"Nope. Sold it and bought a bull." He gestured toward the quiet river. "But we can go fishing here and now."

"We don't have any fishing rods."

"This is the Red River. Catfish." He held up both hands and wiggled his fingers. "Noodling."

"I'm not sticking my arm in a catfish's mouth!"

He laughed. "Had you going for a minute, didn't I?"

She whopped his shoulder. "Get in the boat, cowboy, before I push you in the river."

He stepped onto the flat bottom boat, wobbling a little until he found his balance, and then reached back to help her inside. They settled side by side on one of the two bench boards dividing the boat horizontally. Jake took up both oars, though one was chipped and broken, and pushed away from the bank.

They floated along, barely moving on the gentle current, leaving wide, concentric ripples in their wake. On the water, the air felt cooler and they snuggled together, grinning at the perfect excuse to be close.

"No leaks."

"So far." Allison wrapped her hands around his upper arm and leaned her cheek against his jacket.

Here on the river, alone without the censure of family, she felt such joy. She wanted to discuss their future, to dream of the life they'd have together. Here, on the river in an abandoned rowboat, anything seemed possible.

That Sunday night at her house had changed everything. Now that she knew he loved her, they'd find a way.

"Being with you makes me so happy," she said. Beneath her palms his biceps flexed with every sweep of oar. He tilted his face toward hers, ignoring the direction his oar sent the boat. She saw the worry in his green eyes mixed and mingled with the love.

Other than a few ducks waddling on the shore in search for food, they were the only beings for miles around. Thick trees, though essentially bare, blocked the river from the narrow road where they'd parked the truck before walking down the well-trod path to the sandy shore.

She wanted Jake to say she made him happy, too, but instantly felt childish at the thought. She knew she made him happy. It was there in his laughter, in the tenderness of his hand at the nape of her neck, in the way he perched his cowboy hat on her head and snapped photo after photo with his cell phone. As if he wanted to preserve every moment with her.

Sometimes that scared her, but they'd talked of the future, too. They both wanted a big family and a simple lifestyle. Jake would have a ranch, and in her spare time she'd plan weddings. And if the topic of their own special day never quite arose, Allison didn't worry. Much.

Jake loved her, and in the estimation of great philosophers and poets, but especially in her heart, love conquered all.

Didn't it?

On Thanksgiving Day, cheerful noise and generalized chaos reigned in the Buchanon household. The twins had invited their latest girlfriends. Jayla brought a guy none of them had ever seen before, and Brady arrived with a family he'd been helping to add to the five people their mother had invited, all with nowhere else to go for the holiday. The smells of turkey and sage and pecan pie had the noncooking parties roaming in and out of the kitchen like prowling wolves.

Allison savored the warmth of family more than ever this holiday, wondering if she'd be here for the next one. By the time the dishes were cleared and the crowd had settled in for the traditional football game, she was eager to head to the Hamilton house.

Alone in the kitchen with her mother while the other women checked the house for last-minute dishes and messes, she said quietly, "I'm going home, Mom."

Her mother turned from putting a pie in the refrigerator, her hazel eyes understanding. "Home? Or to Jake's?"

Her mother's tone held no censure, for which Allison was grateful. "Their dinner is tonight. I told Jake I'd help cook. I'm going, Mama." Regardless.

A beat passed while her mother studied her, and then Karen handed over a foil-covered pan. "Take this. Jake always liked my pecan pie."

The lump in Allison's throat melted into tears she swallowed. "I love you, Mama."

But she loved Jake Hamilton, too.

Later than night, full of roast hen, Stove Top stuffing and Mama's pie, Allison and Jake put up a Christmas tree in the front window of the Hamilton house. The artificial pine had been in storage so long they'd had to clean off cobwebs first, but once the lights were on the dust was forgotten.

Cooking dinner together had been fun. Decorating the tree together was even more so. Allison couldn't help dreaming that someday the tree would be their own.

Miss Pat bossed from her chair, which Jake had dubbed the queen's throne, but despite her sass, the older woman had grown quietly nostalgic at the appearance of certain ornaments.

"My mother—that'd be your great-grandma—gave us that little red wagon the year your daddy was born," she said. "His name is engraved on the bottom."

Reverently, Jake turned the ornament in his hand. "I wish I remembered him better. All I remember is how sick he was."

"You were the apple of his eye."

Allison's chest ached as she listened to the exchange between grandson and grandmother, aware they shared a sorrow she couldn't understand. Her family had always been there for her, completely intact, alive and well, and her memories ran deeper than the river.

She felt almost ashamed of how perfect her world had been.

Jake hung the ornament on a limb and reached into the tattered cardboard box for another. She joined him, and soon the melancholy moment passed. When the tree was decorated and the lights blinked a rainbow of colors, she helped Miss Pat to bed, pleased when Jake's grandmother did most of the work herself.

She was on the mend.

When Allison returned to the living room, Jake sat cross-legged on the floor in front the tree, cups of cocoa on a nearby table. She sat down beside him.

"Will you help me with my tree tomorrow?" she asked.

"Need my expertise, huh?"

"Something like that. I put up a real tree. They're harder."

"Wouldn't know. Never had one."

"Don't you put one up in your trailer?"

"No. What's the point? If I'm home at all, I'm the only one there."

"That's sad. I'm the only one in my duplex, but I'll have a tree."

"You have someone to share it with."

The loneliness in that statement struck her. Jake, for nine years, alone in his trailer at Christmas.

He must have read her expression because he said, "Don't feel sorry for me, Allison. I'm not lonely. I'm not sad. I'm usually working at Christmas. No big deal."

It was a big deal to her. And this year, he was home, and she'd see to it that he had the best Christmas ever.

Thanksgiving had filled him in more places than his belly. He'd loved every minute with Allison. Like a dry sponge, he wanted to soak her up, to hold on for the ride and pray the eight-second buzzer never came. He knew he was being foolish, but he couldn't seem to help himself. He should let her go now and get it over with.

Yes, he loved her. But he'd lost enough people who were supposed to love him to know an emotion wasn't enough. His mama had proved as much long before the Buchanons had turned their backs.

So, he spent his days working for Manny, but as soon as the clock struck five, he started obsessing about Allison. Was she home from work? Would she enjoy a movie or a burger? Would she rather hang out at home or maybe take another drive down by the river?

He marked the last idea off his list.

Their last trips to the river had been dangerous. He'd kissed her too many times until he'd seriously considered a dip in the cold river to bring him to his senses. Neither of them could afford for things to get out of hand.

Allison. His whole world had turned in on that one little person with the big brown eyes and flyaway hair.

Since Thanksgiving his mood swung from joy to despair. Joy that she loved him. Despair that they would never work out.

As much as Jake liked the idea, he wouldn't take her with him. They would probably be ecstatically happy for a while in the full bloom of love, but eventually, she'd miss her home, her job, her loved ones. She'd grow to resent the man who'd taken her away from everything that mattered. If her family was broken like his, maybe they'd have a chance, but the Buchanons were different—a powerful, connected whole made stronger by the sum of its individual members. Allison was a link in that chain and she'd crumble without the rest.

He'd interviewed an older widow from elder services

who, like his grandmother, could no longer afford to live alone. She seemed eager to move in with Granny Pat and the invisible Ralph, eager to be a companion and helpmate in exchange for a roof over her head. Jake hadn't told the woman about the mortgage. Saw no need. He was going to pay it one way or the other.

Granny wasn't too keen on live-in help, but she would come around. With Flo on hand as watchdog and general rabble-rouser, Granny Pat had come further in a couple of months than in all the months in rehab.

"I don't need some old woman living in my house."

"Melba's younger than you are, Granny Pat."

"What about my trip to Mexico? I don't have to take her along, do I?"

"She can keep the home fires burning while you're gone."

"You sure are eager to get away from your old grandma."

He knelt beside her chair. Her feet stuck straight out in front of her on the recliner, fuzzy slippers dangling on her skinny white heels. In a lot of ways his tiny grandmother reminded him of Allison. Strong, sassy, small as a child and with the heart of a lioness.

"You know that's not true. If life had turned out differently, I'd never leave. I'd buy land here, close to you, and raise my bulls."

"Always running away. Like your mama. If things get tough, you run."

His hackles rose, shocked by the accusation. "I'm not running away." And he was nothing like his mama. "My being here causes problems. I hurt the Buchanons. They shouldn't have to look at me if they don't want to."

"What about Allison?"

Some of the starch leaked out of him. Allison. His biggest problem. "She'll get hurt the most if I stick around, and a man has to make a living. I can't do that here."

"She'll be hurt if you leave. Money comes and goes. Love's the only thing that lasts."

Now she was a philosopher.

"A responsible man does what's right regardless of what he wants." He was tired of this conversation. Tired of arguing with her and himself and Allison. Tired of trying to squeeze pennies, of dodging Buchanons, of tossing and turning half the night trying to solve the unsolvable.

No matter what his grandmother thought, sometimes a man had to cut his losses and leave the table.

"I'm sorry, Granny P., but the invitation to live with me is still open."

"And I still say no. You're not there half the time. At least here I have friends and neighbors to break up the monotony." She patted his head the way she had when he'd been a lonely, confused little boy clinging to her apron and wondering why his mama had left him. "I'll be fine. You don't get much finer than dancing the samba on the beaches of Mexico."

Jake's mouth twitched. "The samba?"

"Flo's teaching me, and if you're not real careful, I'll come back from Mexico with a new grandpa for you."

"What about Ralph?"

"Jacob Hamilton, you know good and well Ralph is as dead as a hammer."

Jake leaned back on his bootheels and laughed until he tumbled onto his backside. The fall tickled Granny so much she fell into a coughing fit that left her breathless. But the twinkle in her eye told Jake she was going to be fine without him.

He worried about her, but then he worried about everything these days. Granny. Allison. Manny. The confounded mortgage. So many of the people he cared about were here in Gabriel's Crossing.

He wanted to stay, a truth that surprised him. Though he'd never intended to return, being here changed him. Everyone he loved was here. Even his bulls were here.

Jake made a wry face. The bulls were here unless he sold them, a prospect that grew more real every time he spoke to Ned Butterman. Like this morning when the loose-jowled banker had shaken his head in sympathy and promised to hold off on foreclosure until after the New Year.

The trailer in Stephenville could be sold—it was just a place to hang his hat when he wasn't on the road. He warmed to the idea. The small mobile home wasn't much but a sale would bring enough cash to buy his grandmother some time at the bank.

He could move home with Granny Pat for good. She'd like that. And he could figure out a way to avoid the Buchanons most of the time.

Except for Allison. As long as he was in Gabriel's Crossing, he'd seek her out. He could no more ignore her than sprout wings and fly across the Atlantic.

The angst curled in his gut. He loved her too much to leave. He loved her too much to stay.

He sat down on the couch and put his head in his hands. What was he going to do?

Chapter Thirteen

Faith was back, and with enormous relief Allison talked to her friend about Jake and all the craziness with her brothers.

"You're glowing," Faith said while Allison bounced around her bedroom tossing clothes onto the bed.

"That was supposed to be my line." Allison spun in a circle. "Look at you. Tanned and gorgeous and wildly in love."

"True. At least the tanned and in love part. And Derrick thinks I'm gorgeous."

"He's a smart fellow. I'm so glad you came home for a few days while he settled the business in Oklahoma."

"I needed to pack up a few more things anyway. Besides, I miss everyone."

"You have to visit often."

"We will." She put her aqua handbag on a chair, folding the strap on top. "Why are you throwing clothes everywhere like a mad thing?"

"Jake's taking me somewhere special. He said to dress up because it's a surprise."

Faith squealed. "This sounds promising."

"I know! I'm so excited." A secret hope kept sprouting up like a dandelion, both beautiful and unwanted. She wondered if Jake would propose. "Up until now, he's stubbornly insisted we'd be miserable together."

"Would you be?"

"No, of course not." Allison chewed her bottom lip as she contemplated a brown skirt.

"Are you sure?"

"Now you sound like Jake."

Faith pushed away the skirt. "Try this red one with the lace top. The flared hemline is adorable, and you'll look amazing in red heels."

Allison held the garment to her waist. "Oh, yeah. This one."

"Any progress with the family?"

"About Jake? No. Except for Dawson. He's softening."

"Dawson's always been a soft touch where you're concerned."

"He's a good brother."

"They all are, Allison. They love you and they're afraid you'll get hurt. They're afraid of losing you."

Allison knew that. Sometimes she was afraid, too. Afraid of losing them, of losing Jake again. Both scared her no end.

"Love will find a way." She had to believe that to keep breathing. "Will you do my nails?"

Faith flexed her fingers. "Put yourself into my capable hands, my dear. I will make you beautiful."

By the time Jake arrived, Faith had headed to her mother's house, but not before she'd overseen every detail of Allison's beauty routine. With her hair flipped and fluffed, her nails sparkling red to match her skirt and shoes and her makeup carefully applied, she felt like a new woman.

Apparently, Jake agreed.

"Wow," he said when she opened the door. "Glad I brought these." He pulled a small bouquet of red roses from behind his back.

Allison squealed. "They're beautiful."

"So are you."

Okay, this was going to be a great night. In her heels, she almost reached his chin and with little effort, tiptoed up and smacked his lips with hers.

His grin widened. "Remind me to bring roses more often."

She liked the sound of that. Jake looked handsome in the same sport jacket he'd worn to Faith's wedding and a pea-green shirt that darkened the black circles around his green irises. "Let me put these in water."

He plucked one rose from the many and held it beneath his nose for a long sniff. "One for the road."

While she placed the flowers in a vase, they flirted and teased. Allison could barely keep her eyes off him and she knew he felt the same because every time she glanced his way, he was staring at her with a half smile.

There was mystery and romance in the air, a night of possibilities. And Allison couldn't wait to discover what was on his mind.

Jake was aware of the quiet conversations going on at the nearby tables and the quieter swish of waiters moving through the dining room. He was glad he'd chosen this restaurant even if it strained his weeping budget. Allison deserved nice things and beautiful places.

He loved her, and he wanted to give her the world, but he had little to offer. Nothing really but hard work and heartache. A man of courage would get in his truck and drive away, but Granny Pat was right. He was afraid. Not of the Buchanon brothers, but of shriveling away to nothing, a broken down rodeo bum whose heart had withered and died without his one true love.

He looked across the table at her. She was beautiful in

the amber glow of candlelight, this woman who'd begun healing him at seventeen and never stopped.

By the end of the evening, Jake was fighting both his head and his heart. He'd known this date would take a toll, but after all the times he'd failed her on so many levels, he wanted to do this right. Splurge a little. Buy her roses and treat her to a beautiful dinner and a good time. Show his love in the only ways he could.

During his times away from her, the situation was clear. He had to leave. He loved her too much to separate her from her family. But being with her muddled his thinking. Her Pollyanna effect seeped into him and had him wondering if there was a better way.

She reached across the flickering candle and dabbed a napkin against his cheek. "Cheesecake."

"I was saving it for it later."

"Ha. Funny." She leaned back in the chair, fingertips on her stomach and tried for a deep breath. "That was amazingly good. I'm too stuffed to breathe."

"Me, too. Want to take a walk?" He tossed his napkin beside his plate. "There's a park not far from here. The Christmas displays are supposed to be nice."

"Walk? I don't know if I can move!" But she rose when he came around to hold her chair. "You know I'm a sucker for Christmas lights."

Yeah, and he was a sucker for her.

In the foyer, he helped her into her coat and guided her through the parking lot, relishing the soft warmth of her hand in his. He was a Texas boy, raised with manners, but a long time had passed since he'd taken such pleasure in doting on a woman.

He wanted it to always be this way. He wanted her to be his forever, and the wanting clawed a raw place in his soul.

* * *

The park was Christmas in all its glory, though the night was cold and their breaths froze in puffs of fog as they strolled through the displays. Allison snuggled close to Jake's side, breathing in the pleasure of his woodsy cologne and the frosty air. Every naked tree lifted its branches in a lace-sleeved welcome of white lights beneath a starless sky overwhelmed by the earthly radiance.

Though others braved the chill, Allison felt cocooned in a world that included only the two of them. No outside problems. No family conflict. Just a man and woman in love. Was this the way it would be if they lived away from Gabriel's Crossing?

"Faith is back from her honeymoon," she said.

"I guess they had a great time."

"The best. She says Saint Thomas is a fabulous place, especially this time of year. Her photos are incredible. I can't imagine water that blue or beaches as white."

"Our water is red and so are the beaches. We're river rats."

Allison shivered, though the cold was only part of the reason. She didn't know why the memory pressed in on her tonight. Maybe the mention of the reddish sand or the fact that they'd not spoken of that awful event at all. Now, here, miles away from her volatile brothers, she wasn't afraid to bring up the subject.

"I should have told them what happened that night at the river with Terry," she said softly. "Maybe things would have been different for you."

Beside her, Jake stiffened. He paused in midstride and turned toward her. "I'd hoped you'd forgotten."

"A girl doesn't forget a lesson like that. If you hadn't been there…" She shook her head. "I never should have gone off with him. I knew he had a wild reputation."

"Why did you?"

"You." She hunched her shoulders, recalling that night on the river. A group of them had built a bonfire and were hanging out after a football game. She didn't realize Terry was drinking until it was too late. "I was angry at my parents because of you."

"I was pretty angry myself." He took her hand and chafed it between both of his. "That's why I was there in the first place."

"All by yourself at the river." Regret and sadness poked at her. He'd been so alone back then after the accident, when no one wanted to hang out with him. Except her, and she'd been forbidden. After the incident that night she'd refused to listen to her family on the subject of Jake, but sneaking around had never been her style either.

"I didn't know your group of friends would show up," he said. "When I heard the voices, I moseyed on down the riverbank and around the bend, away from the bonfire."

"You must have despised all of us, down there having fun while you were left out."

"I deserved it, Allison. The same way Terry deserved a busted nose."

The images had stayed with her, as vivid now as ever. Her torn clothes, the struggle there on the red sand, her pleas for mercy that only made Terry more aggressive, the wrenching sobs she couldn't stop. And always the image of her hero, of Jake taking on the bigger boy, of throwing his coat over her exposed body and carrying her to his truck.

"I don't like to think what would have happened if you hadn't been there."

"I was scared of what he'd done."

"Me, too." She touched his cheek. "Thank God, as ugly as it was, it wasn't the worst. I was terrified of what my brothers would do if they found out."

Jake captured her fingers against his chilly skin, brought them to his lips and kissed them. A thrill raced through her.

"That's the only reason I agreed with your idea to keep the whole mess a secret. You were so upset. The way you cried for hours scared me. I would have agreed to anything to make you feel better again. Your family had been through so much with Quinn, and he was still recovering. Knowing what Terry tried to do might have sent them over the edge."

"I was afraid they'd do something terrible and end up in jail. Especially Brady with his temper."

"They might have. I certainly wanted to."

"I think I should tell them now."

He tilted his head to one side. "What good could possibly come from that?"

"You. I know my brothers. They'd respect what you did. The way you helped me."

"No." He gripped her fingers tighter. "Don't go there, Allison. Don't rip open a hornet's nest at this late date. Not on my behalf."

"I want them to accept you, Jake. As the man I love, the man who was there for me when they weren't."

"And what if you tell them and nothing changes? What if you open up a can of worms and they do something crazy. Aren't you concerned about that? Terry has a wife and family and seems to be a solid citizen now."

"You checked him out?"

He shrugged. "Had to. Didn't want that to happen to any other woman."

Jake's strong arm came around her. "As much as I wanted to drown the guy for hurting you, you were right when you asked me to keep the secret. Your family didn't need more grief."

"I thought so then." Now she wasn't so sure. Now, she worried her humiliation had been the motivator, not her concern for her brothers.

Jake bundled her close to his side. "You're freezing. Come on, let's head for the truck. Want to stop somewhere for hot chocolate?"

"Jake," she said, frustrated.

He touched his lips to the top of her head and in a quietly pleading voice, said, "Not tonight, okay? Just let it go."

She got the message. He wouldn't let her try to make him a hero in her brothers' eyes.

"Okay. For now." She put her hand over his heart and whispered. "You've always been my hero."

"Ah, Allison." His chest rose and fell in a quiet sigh. When she tipped her chin up, he kissed her. With the cold air swirling and a snowman display singing "Frosty the Snowman" in a tinny, animated voice, Allison let herself revel in his embrace.

Jake bewildered her at times. If he loved her, why wouldn't he do whatever he could to make things right with her family? Why wouldn't he take a chance when their future together hung in the balance?

But of course, she didn't have answers any more than she ever had. That had been their dilemma for nearly ten years.

Jake thought his chest would crack open with love for his special lady. He was no hero, but she made him feel like one.

He didn't understand why Allison had brought up the subject of that night on the river, an incident he'd buried as deeply as possible. No man wanted pictures in his head of the woman he loved being attacked by another man. Thinking about Terry Dean still had the power to infuriate him to the point of combustion. Didn't she understand that her brothers would feel the same?

Telling them wouldn't resolve a thing. It would only cause more trouble.

Slowly, he pulled away from the tender embrace, holding her perhaps an extra moment longer than was wise. If he had his way, he'd never let go. He'd stand right here in a Sherman, Texas, park until he turned into a Popsicle.

"What do you want for Christmas?" he asked.

She cocked her head and her dark hair took flight in a fickle puff of arctic air. "Are you going to buy me a present?"

He could see she was delighted. "Depends on my wallet and the size of what you want."

"A Mercedes-Benz."

"Done. With a big red bow on the hood."

They both laughed. A Mercedes was as unlikely as paying the mortgage on time.

"What would you like?"

You. But he didn't say that. "To take you to church on Christmas Eve."

"Jake, that is so sweet. I'd love to. But I still want to buy you a gift. Tell me something."

"You can give me your accounting medal. I think I may need it."

Allison's hitching laugh rang out. Glad they'd moved away from the unpleasant topic of Terry Dean, Jake took her hand and they sauntered on through the park sharing silly gift ideas. They admired the displays, laughed at some, including a moving dinosaur wearing a Santa hat.

"That's what I want for Christmas," Jake declared.

"What? A wire-framed dinosaur?"

"No, the Santa hat!"

By the time they reached the truck, chilled to the toenails, lips frozen and teeth chattering, their mood was light and fun and Jake almost believed in the impossible.

While he fished in his pocket for the truck key with Allison dancing around him and peppering him with silly ideas and quick, cold kisses, a cell phone rang from inside her tiny clutch bag.

"Hold that thought," she said and then giggled as she whipped out the device and answered.

"Oh, hi." Her smile faded. Her energetic bounce calmed.

"Who—?" he started to ask, but her eyes flicked a warning and she turned slightly to the side. That one little motion jabbed like rejection.

What was that all about?

Tense now, his bubble of joy burst, he busied himself with unlocking the truck. The dome light illuminated them, a weak spill of white that turned her lacy blouse ghostly pale.

"Looking at Christmas lights," he heard her say. Then the air quivered with hesitation. She glanced at him again, and this time her brown eyes pled for understanding as she said, "Just a friend."

Those three little words ripped his heart out and left him bloody and beaten and as cold as the winter night. She wanted to free him with her brothers, but she wasn't ready to tell anyone they'd had dinner together.

Jake started the truck. He shouldn't be upset. He had no right to be, but his heart hurt just the same.

Allison knew the phone call had hurt him. With her throat thick with regret, she put her phone away and climbed inside the truck.

"I should have told him." She touched his arm. A muscle flexed, tensed, held rigid.

"You did the right thing, all things considered."

Had she? Was hiding her love for Jake to avoid confrontation the "right thing"?

They'd had a perfect evening, full of special moments and romance and wonderful food. For this brief spell of time the future had been theirs.

Why did Dad have to call anyway? But worse, why hadn't she had the courage to simply tell her father the truth? That she was on a date with Jake and loving every minute with him.

Because she was a bigger coward than she'd thought. Because she didn't want to rock the boat. Because her family's disapproval wore on her.

Every reason shamed her. Jake was a good man, worthy of the words *I love you.* Yet, what kind of love turned away in the face of adversity?

During the drive home, Jake said all the right things in response to her chatter, but he was different. Wounded. Because of her and her family. As usual.

No wonder he wanted to get away. All they'd ever done was hurt him.

Long after midnight they arrived at her duplex. Jayla's side of the home was dark, and Allison was relieved, another reason to feel ashamed. Allison didn't want to have that discussion. More than once, her younger sister had warned her to be careful.

Right. She'd been so careful she'd stabbed Jake in the back in a simple phone call.

"Want to come in?" she asked, huddled in her coat, wishing he'd hold her.

In the dark yard with little more than a pale wash from the corner streetlight, Jake's face was in shadow. "It's late."

"Are you mad at me, Jake?" She stepped closer, toward the warmth of his breathing. "I'll tell Dad we were together."

"I'm not mad. You did the right thing."

"No, I didn't. I hurt you and that's never right. I love you, Jake."

He was silent for a bit, his hands deep in his pockets, the brim of his hat tilted out toward the darkness.

"I wanted to give you tonight," he finally murmured.

Something in his tone set her nerves jumping. "Tonight was wonderful. I had the best time."

"Good." He brought his gaze down to hers and nodded once. "Good."

"Jake, are we okay?"

He didn't answer and her anxiety increased. He tugged his hands from his pockets and caressed her face. "You deserve the best, Allison. The very best."

While she grappled to understand his meaning, he kissed her forehead, his lips lingering for a long moment. Then he stepped off her porch and disappeared into the darkness.

Goodbyes stunk. Jake vowed to remember that the next time around.

Hat in hand, he stood inside Manny's big silver barn. While he'd told his friend of his plans, Paulina had fed him, and then Manny had insisted on riding with him to check on the animals. The rancher refused to stay down. He forked hay with the tractor, mixed the special brand of feed reserved for the bucking stock and continued ranching with few exceptions. A bum knee would never keep Manny Morales down for long.

"The only thing I can't do yet is fix fence and load bulls. Soon, though. Soon."

"Tim should be able to handle that until you're ready."

"*Sí.* He's a good hand. Reminds me of you at that age."

"Tell him to keep his nose clean and not to be stupid."

Manny's teeth flashed. "You tell him yourself. He comes every day even if I don't need him."

"You're good for him. Like you were for me."

"You're staying through Christmas, aren't you? 'Cause if you don't, you gonna break Paulina's heart."

"I'll do my best."

"What you got in Stephenville that's better than here?" Not a thing. "The neighbors like me better."

"Paulina and me, we pray for you about this. We pray for the Buchanons, too. They are a fine family but they have a burr in their saddle. Only God can pluck it out."

"Maybe this is my cross to bear, Manny. My penance for the stupid things I've done."

"Maybe. But my heart says no. Why you think they call Jesus the Prince of Peace. Huh? He tells us not to have bad feelings toward others. You keep praying."

Jake clapped his old friend on the back. "I'll do that. Fact of the matter, I thought I'd take a walk down to my bulls. I pray better with the smell of manure in my nose."

Manny let out a hearty laugh. "Well, go on. Go see your sons. This weather won't last much longer."

Jake raised a hand in agreement as he stepped out into the afternoon. The early December sky was as gray and shiny as a new nickel. He considered driving the Polaris but opted for a head-clearing walk. The air held a chill, but he didn't mind. His coat was warm and forty acres wasn't far for a man with a lot of praying to do. Boots scuffing the dead grass, he opened one gate after another until the house disappeared from sight. About a dozen brood cows saw him and ambled along behind, bawling when he had no feed bucket.

With the cows in hot pursuit, he stopped at his favorite little pond where Jake spotted deer and turkey tracks. The water reminded him of Allison and their day in the borrowed boat. A sweet day, a day that would linger in his memory like the taste of sugar.

"Give her every good thing, Lord," he murmured.

As if in response, one of the cows stuck her wet snout against his back and snuffled. Jake jumped, then laughed at himself. The others ambled away, bored with a human who didn't feed them.

He settled on a rock and prayed a little but no revelations flashed from the heavens. He started on, feeling defeated. He considered writing Allison a letter to tell her everything that was in his heart, but perhaps a phone call would be better. No, not a call. Hearing her voice would ruin him.

Head down, he prayed as he walked, searching for answers that didn't come. Granny Pat said he was running away like his mother. But she was wrong. He was doing the Christian thing. Turning the other cheek. Walking away from the fight. Wasn't that what Jesus had done?

Something Manny said nudged him. Jesus was all about peace and love and caring for each other. Did that mean he wasn't being punished for the bad choices he'd made as a kid? He wasn't sure and even if he was, it wouldn't change anything. The Buchanons would still despise his name. Allison would still be caught in the middle. But pondering the idea encouraged him.

As he neared his bull pasture and the loading pens where Manny worked the cattle, he heard excited voices. Going on alert, he strained toward the sound. Had those kids come back here after being warned away more than once?

Hurrying now, he drew nearer, and his suspicions were confirmed. Only this time the situation was far worse. The two young boys, one dark and one fair, had maneuvered several bulls into the loading corrals, and one of the boys had climbed atop the iron gate preparing to step onto the back of the bull. Jake's blood ran cold. For a second he froze, too afraid for the kid to think. But then his bull rider training kicked in and adrenaline jacked into his system so fast his vision blurred.

"Hey, you boys!" He started to run though his legs felt like Jell-O. As in a dream, he seemed to run without making progress. "Get out of there. Now!"

But the boys either didn't hear or refused to listen. They were focused on the bulls and the exciting adventure.

Jake was less than twenty yards away when the blond boy—Charity's boy, he now saw with terrible clarity—slipped his leg over the bull and disaster broke loose. The bull, feeling the presence of a human for the first time, went ballistic, thrashing and slinging his massive, horned head.

Fear slammed Jake, a metallic sting that tore through his blood vessels.

"Oh, God," was the only prayer he had time for.

The boy lasted two seconds before the big Brahma, nearly grown and ready for the ring, kicked out from behind and made one mighty jerk. In other circumstances, Jake would have been proud of his young bucking bull.

All he could think of was getting to Ryan before the bull did.

His boots slowed him down. His breath came in short gasps.

One of the boys screamed, his jubilance turning to a cry of terror. Jake didn't know which boy had cried out but Ryan lay facedown on the ground inside the small pen… And a massive, angry bull headed straight for him.

The next moments occurred in slow motion. Jake struggled to move faster. His heart hammered against his ribcage.

He yelled, trying to startle the bull away from the boy, but he was too late.

As he reached the gate, the bull hooked Ryan's inert body and tossed him high into the air.

Jake knew that feeling of going airborne. He also knew the crash was not worth the ride. His stomach sickened.

The other boy, clinging to the top of the corral, screamed again. Ryan's body hit the hard December ground with a terrifying thud and he lay still.

"Ryan. Move!" Jake yelled. "Crawl toward your friend."

But Ryan didn't move.

The bull, enraged now and probably as frightened as the boys, charged the injured Ryan again.

Fueled on reaction and adrenaline, Jake bolted over the gate and ran toward the bull. Yelling, he flailed his arms. The animal ignored the man in favor of the child. He pushed his fierce head against Ryan's body.

As he'd seen bullfighters do dozens of times in the arena, Jake grabbed the mighty horns to divert the bull's attention away from the fallen child. The angry animal whipped around and came for him. Jake dodged, but the bull caught his side. He went down hard, tasted blood and dirt, but popped up again. His side burned like a welding torch. But as long as the bull focused on him, Ryan had a chance to get away.

He ran toward the bull again.

"Get up, Ryan," he yelled. He didn't have time to consider the alternative. Maybe Ryan couldn't get up.

He yanked his hat from his head and slapped at the massive head. The bull turned on him.

The smell of dust and manure choked him. His ears rang and his head swam. He shook off the sensation, fighting for clarity. Fighting for Ryan's life. And his own.

"Mister. Mister! The gate."

Thank God.

Escape.

The dark-haired kid had the presence of mind to provide an escape route.

Though breathless and hurting, Jake loped toward the open gate with the bull too close behind him. One misstep, he'd go down and the bull would be upon him. The moment Big Country passed through the opening Jake leaped up on the iron railing beside the kid and slammed the gate onto its latch. His bull was loose in the wrong pasture but that could be rectified now that the boys were safe.

The thought no more than hit his brain than Jake leaped down and raced toward Ryan. The boy remained on the ground, inert.

Jake fell to his knees beside the child. "Ryan. Ryan. It's Jake Hamilton. Can you hear me?"

The boy didn't respond. A new terror, far more frightening than the Brahma, ricocheted through Jake. What if Charity's boy died?

He put shaky fingers against Ryan's throat and nearly collapsed with relief to feel a pulse. The boy was alive. For now.

The adrenaline rush pounded through him with such power, he trembled like a wet Chihuahua. He shook his head to clear away the fear and dust and dizziness.

He ripped his cell phone from his pocket and punched 9-1-1. In this remote town, the call went straight to Gabriel's Crossing's fire and rescue. He identified himself and explained the situation.

What he learned shook him even worse.

"All the emergency vehicles are out on a call. It'll be a couple of hours."

"Two hours!" Two hours when a boy's life hung in the balance. "He can't wait that long."

"Sorry, Jake, there's a big car wreck out on Highway 7. We can't get there any faster. If you can move the patient, you'd best bring him to town yourself."

He was forty acres from his truck and three miles from town. His side screamed and he was dizzy.

But Ryan was bleeding from his nose and mouth.

After a quick call to Manny, he gently braced the child's neck as much as possible, scooped him up and began to run. Once again, Buchanon blood was on his hands.

Jake paced the emergency waiting area of Gabriel's Crossing's hospital. The car accident victims had come in about the same time he'd arrived with Ryan. One harried doctor and a handful of scrub-clad nurses rushed in and out of rooms while techs pushed carts bearing machinery and IV tubes in a mad dash against too many simultaneous disasters. Their little hospital was unprepared for this much action.

The single elevator pinged so many times, Jake stopped looking that direction. A small tabletop television next to a Mr. Coffee machine rolled *Fox News,* but the only news he wanted was that Charity's son would be all right. So far, all he'd done was pace and worry. The Buchanons, alerted by the hospital less than five minutes ago, had yet to arrive. He was thankful he'd not been the one to call them.

The acrid smell of Ryan's blood burned in his nostrils. Still-moist blood stained his blue shirt. Jake looked way from the sight in search of something, anything to take his mind off the memory of Ryan's terrible stillness, his limp, pale form and the free flow of warm, sticky blood.

His gaze landed on Chet, Ryan's cohort. The dark-haired boy had sat in Jake's truck cab, his lower lip trembling, his skin almost as white as Ryan's and said nothing during the short, but endless, drive to the E.R.

Ryan's cohort. Subsequent attempts at conversation resulted in shrugs and crossed arms, trembling lips and a mulish glare. Jake recognized the symptoms. The kid was scared out of his mind. Jake's attempts at reassurance fell flat. After all, what did he know? Ryan was unconscious and bleeding. He couldn't promise Chet that his buddy would be all right.

He felt for the kid, though he wanted to blast him, too, for pulling such a dangerous stunt. But pity won out, and Jake cut him a break and left him alone. Time enough to sort out the blame. Jake knew plenty about that, too.

Being in this waiting room with an injured Buchanon flashed him back to that horrible day when he'd brought Quinn in, bleeding and pale as death. Like Ryan.

He shuddered. No use going back to the worst day of his life.

But the images kept coming. The Buchanons' frightened faces. Karen and the girls in a huddle, crying. Dan threatening to tear the place down brick by brick if someone didn't tell him something fast. Then there were the brothers, the men he'd come to think of as his own siblings. They'd stood together near the women, brawny arms crossed, faces tight, blocking him out. Even in those first moments they had blamed him, though no more than he'd blamed himself.

He'd sat with his head in his hands talking to the sheriff, alone and scared spitless, sure he'd go to prison forever, sure his best friend would die. Wishing he was in that exam room instead of Quinn.

He raked a hand down his face and shook his head to dispel the images. So much tragedy, all with his name attached.

Now there was Ryan, another member of the Buchanon

family, though Jake thanked God that, other than owning the bull, he'd had nothing to do with this incident.

Suddenly, Chet leaped from his speckled plastic chair and rushed across the room. Jake looked up to see Charity, Brady and Quinn hurrying down the hallway with Karen and Dan not far behind.

Charity rushed toward the intake window with Karen at her side. Jake could hear them murmuring to the familiar-looking receptionist in hushed, frantic tones. He wanted to go to them and tell them what he knew and offer reassurances. He didn't. Couldn't. He wouldn't be welcome, just as he'd not been welcomed into the tight circle of Buchanons the day Quinn was shot.

He considered a trip to the restroom to check out the pain in his side, but opted against it. He'd been tossed around in the ring before. He'd survive.

He prayed Ryan did.

So, he took a seat at the far end of the waiting area and kept out of the way, letting the family take care of the necessary paperwork he'd known nothing about. When they were ready, they'd ask and he'd tell them what he knew.

Like the outsider he was, Jake watched them talk to the doctor, ached when Charity fell weeping into her mother's arms, and longed to ask what was going on. But he didn't. Though he couldn't leave until he knew something, he wasn't welcome in their conversations either.

More families, apparently from the car accident, crowded into the waiting room waiting for news of their loved ones. Jake gave his seat to a woman holding a small baby and went to stand against the wall. The hushed, tense conversations unnerved him. Ryan's blood felt sticky against his chest.

Opposite him, Quinn and Brady talked to Chet, and from Chet's teary eyes and frightened expression, he was relating the incident. Better the boy told of the misdeeds than for the news to come from Jake.

When Allison burst into the crowded waiting room Jake's stomach lifted. Brown eyes wide with worry, she beelined to her mother and Charity for supportive hugs. She didn't see him standing apart, holding up this wall. Ryan was the focus, the one who mattered, not Jake and his tattered relationship with her family. Still, having her in the room buoyed him.

While Jake's focus was on Allison, Quinn stormed across the waiting room and pushed into his space. "You worthless scum. Chet told us what you did. You moron."

Tense and wary, Jake cut a gaze toward the boy. "Exactly what did he tell you?"

"Don't play dumb. You have no business teaching these boys how to ride a bull."

"Do what?"

But Quinn was in no mood to explain. Before Jake knew what was coming, a hard fist smashed into his jaw. Jake's head jerked back, slammed the wall. His hat tumbled to the gray tile floor. Dark stars exploded behind his eyelids. His knees buckled though he somehow managed to retain his feet.

Like a wounded prize fighter in slo-mo, he shook his head, hand to his jaw. The ache spread up the side of his head into his temple. With his brain rattled, he couldn't comprehend. "What—?"

"Quinn, stop it. Stop it!" From across the room, Allison's distressed voice rang out and called attention to the confrontation. A dull flush of shame suffused Jake. Simply by being here, he'd caused a problem for all of them.

If he'd needed confirmation to leave Gabriel's Crossing sooner rather than later, he'd just received it.

Jake refused to look toward Allison. This wasn't her fight or her problem.

Quinn bowed up, the quarterback with his game face on, serious and eager for contact. "Come on, cowboy, don't just stand there. Be a man."

Jake struggled to keep his voice low and even. The old Jake wanted to retaliate as he'd done that night to Terry Dean. He wanted to put his fist in Quinn's face and prove his worth. But the new Jake understood the truth. Every action had repercussions. The same as in bull riding. A slight move to the left or right and a man would end up with his face in the dirt and a no-ride.

He didn't need any more no-rides in his life. "I told you before, Quinn. I won't do this. Not here. Not ever."

But Quinn had no compunction about coming at him again.

Brady grabbed his brother's fist. "Not here, bro."

Fury reddened Quinn's face. His fist remained tight and upraised as he strained against his brother, eager to land one more blow to his enemy's face.

Enemy.

The reason was skewed, but his former friend had every right to take his anger out on Jake. Manny was wrong. Quinn's anger, even his fist, was Jake's penance for the harm he'd done.

"We'll deal with this later." Brady didn't remove his big hand from his brother's good arm, the only arm he could hit with. "Come on. Charity needs our support, not this."

Quinn took one step back, but his glare never left Jake's face. "You're not wanted here."

In his peripheral vision Jake saw Allison moving toward them along with the rest of the Buchanons. It was the Buchanon way. When one had a problem, they all did. In Allison's case, she was caught between the two, trapped as she would be forever if he didn't get out of her life once and for all.

He wanted to tell her to back off, to stay out of his problems but knew she wouldn't listen. There was only one way to protect her from these confrontations. The Buchanons would never let go. So he had to. For Allison.

"I understand." The admission hurt worse than the punch. He wasn't wanted, and yet he'd kept hoping things would change. His beautiful, optimistic Allison had given him hope. But now he accepted the inevitable. Nothing would ever change for him. Not here in Gabriel's Crossing.

His side and jaw throbbed but not as badly as his heart. It killed him to do this, to walk out and leave behind the only woman he would ever love.

"I hope Ryan's all right. I'll be praying for him." Holding his side, he stiffly scooped his hat from the floor and clapped it onto his head.

Then, while Quinn glared holes in his back and with Allison's stunned expression a snapshot in his memory, he walked out of the emergency room and away from everything that had ever really mattered.

Chapter Fourteen

The hospital parking lot, normally half-empty, was packed today. Allison stood in the E.R. entrance beneath the brick awning and frantically cast around for the slender cowboy in a gray Stetson. She hadn't seen his truck when she'd pulled in, but then she'd been so focused on Ryan she'd thought of nothing else. The lack of news about her nephew terrified her, but her brothers just plain made her mad.

What had Quinn been thinking to do such a stupid thing? Such a useless, macho thing as picking a fight in a hospital waiting room?

A north wind whipped a paper cup into noisy somersaults and set Allison's hair and scarf fluttering like wind socks. She searched the lot, finally spotting her cowboy, head down, hands in his pockets, walking in the other direction.

"Jake!" Weaving between tightly jammed vehicles, she sprinted toward him. "Jake!"

He kept moving forward as if her cheerleader voice hadn't carried above the engine noises coming from the adjacent roadway. When he reached his truck and fished for his key fob, Allison darted across the driving lane. A car honked. She squealed and ducked aside, laughing in embarrassment as she gave an "I'm sorry" shrug to the driver. The commotion turned Jake around.

Allison's heart tumbled in her chest. A dark bruise already spread along his jaw and over his cheek. "Oh, Jake."

Breathless from the mad dash across the parking lot, she caught up to him and touched his cheek with her chilled fingers. Expression solemn, Jake turned his head away.

"Go back inside, Allison."

"Quinn shouldn't have done that. I'm so sorry."

"He did what he's needed to do for a long time." He clicked the unlock on his key fob. "I had it coming."

"That's ridiculous. Hitting people resolves nothing." Although, right now, she'd like to knock both their heads together.

His chest heaved in a deep, weary sigh. "Allison, this is hopeless. Let me go. There's no use beating a dead horse. This is never going to work out."

His words packed a chill colder than the north wind. She shivered. "What are you saying?"

"I think you know. You. Me. This crazy notion that we could fall in love and love would make everything all right. I tried to warn you." He shook his head, looked away and back again. "This whole thing has been doomed from the beginning. I should have stuck to the plan, but you came charging in to Granny Pat's with your optimism and—"

A slow slide of fear crawled down her back like a black widow spider. "So this is my fault?"

"No, never. I'm to blame. I always have been. This isn't about you."

"You're scaring me, Jake."

As if her words pained him, he closed his eyes and pulled her against his chest. Relieved, Allison wrapped her arms around him. He gasped, a short suck of air that had her stepping back to look at him. "You're hurt."

"It's nothing."

"Yes, it is. You're pale. Did Quinn do this?"

He shook his head. "The bull."

"The bull that hurt Ryan? I don't understand."

"Never mind. I've had worse. Go back inside." He clenched his teeth. "Go now."

"You're leaving, aren't you?" He didn't have to answer for her to know. He'd had all of her brothers one man could be expected to tolerate. "Take me with you."

"Do you have any idea how much I want to do exactly that? Any idea at all? But I won't." He touched her cheek. His fingers were cold. "You belong with your family, not with me. Go back inside, support your sister and take care of Ryan. It's time for me to get out of the way. If I hit the road now, I can make the rodeo in Fort Worth this weekend."

Her knees started to tremble. "But Christmas…you'll come back."

"I love you, Allison, and because I do—" Smoldering green eyes sad, he smoothed a lock of her hair. "I won't."

Then while she reeled, heart shattering into a million pieces there in the concrete lot of a hospital, Jake stepped up into the cab of the big pickup truck, closed the door and drove away.

Allison stood in the parking lot with all her dreams tumbling down around her like a wobbly stack of bricks. Her mouth dry, her stomach aching, she wanted to scream and rail against the unfairness. She didn't know who made her the angriest, her brothers or Jake. Men could be such idiots.

He loved her, so he was leaving.

Exactly how much sense did that make?

Oh, she understood his reasons. She understood the kind of toll her brothers' animosity had taken on him, especially when he kicked himself more often than they ever could.

She slapped at the tears burning her eyes. He'd made

his choice. And it wasn't her. Oh, but why did her insides feel as if they were collapsing in on her like an imploded building? They could have resolved the problems with her family eventually if he would have given them a chance.

"Allison?" Brady came toward her, his work boots thudding softly against the concrete. "Everything okay out here?"

She, the one who'd told Jake that violence resolved nothing, wanted to kick her big brother in the shins.

Afraid of answering that question lest she fall apart here and now, she asked, "Any word on Ryan?"

He stopped next to her and turned his back to the north, his oversized body shielding her from the crisp wind. "They moved him to ICU. He's still unconscious."

"Oh, Brady." She walked into his chest and when his comforting arms encircled her, she rested against him in relief. Big brother had always been there with a shoulder to lean all, for all of them.

"Hamilton gone?"

She nodded, her cheek rubbing the rough corduroy of his heavy shirt.

"Good riddance. After what he did."

For once, Allison didn't argue or defend. What was the point? Jake was gone, and neither the tragedy from the past or her own heartache mattered in the face of Ryan's injury. "Do you think Ryan will be okay?"

She heard him swallow, felt the rise and fall of his big chest. "They're waiting on more tests. An MRI of his brain when the mobile unit arrives."

"Oh." She made a small whimpering sound.

"Until then, we wait and stay strong. Charity's a basket case."

Allison stepped out of his hug, shivering when the cold

wind replaced Brady's sturdy warmth. "Should we try to contact Trevor?"

"Up to Charity. She needs his support, that's for sure, but if he's on a mission, by the time we get word to him, things may change. Better to wait until we know more."

"What can we do to help her?"

"Be there. Pray. That's what Buchanons do."

Of course. Brady was right. Buchanons didn't abandon one another, even when they were wrong.

Although he drove through Dallas traffic, Jake made the two hour trip with time to kill. He'd stopped at Granny Pat's, only to find her on the way out to senior bingo with Flo and Melba. She'd been laughing, more her old self, so he'd taken the coward's way out, deciding to call her later. She'd known this was coming, that he needed to work and, more than that, he needed to get away.

The ladies had asked about his bloody shirt and bruised jaw, but he'd made vague noises about an encounter with a bull, only half a lie. He'd changed his shirt, downed some aspirin for the pain in his side and face and aimed his ride toward Fort Worth.

He'd expected to feel better with each mile he put between himself and trouble. But he didn't. He'd wrestled with his conscience, with his heart and with the look of betrayal on Allison's face.

He was leaving a mess behind. The mortgage loomed like a black cloud, but he'd call Manny and ask him to sell enough bulls to pay off the house. A secure future was the only thing he could give his grandmother, even if doing so meant putting his own dreams on hold for a few more years.

He wished he'd had something to give Allison. Anything except a broken heart.

In between questioning every decision he'd ever made, he prayed for Ryan. Not knowing worried him. He kept remembering the blood on his shirt and the pale stillness of Ryan's body in his arms. He was just a young boy. A boy who'd made a foolish decision that had cost him too much.

Jake understood all too well.

He still couldn't believe the other kid had lied to the Buchanons about the incident. Why would Chet do that?

But he knew. Or at least, he suspected. Ryan and Chet were privy to Buchanon conversations. Kids were smart. They would know about the hostility between Jake and the Buchanon family. Everyone in Gabriel's Crossing did.

He parked at the Cowtown Coliseum and paid his entry fee to ride both nights. Then he roamed the stockyards and considered a meal at Joe T. Garcia's which only made him think of Allison again and her penchant for hot foods. He decided to save his money.

Frustrated and down, he went back to the Coliseum to hang out with other cowboys. He had to refocus, get his game face on and be prepared to ride. Riding was as much mental as physical. Sometimes more. Anything less could get him killed.

Afternoon turned to evening. Hospital shifts changed and a new group of nurses came on duty. Like the previous staff, most of them knew the Buchanon family who crowded the hospital room and overflowed into the hallway and waiting area. No one had the heart or the nerve to ask them to leave. They all understood the Buchanons would stay until Ryan was out of the woods.

A weepy, shaky Charity was hugged over and over by visitors who'd heard the news and who'd come to express their concern. Chet's mother arrived and sat with her son who begged to stay until he could see Ryan. Pastor and

Mrs. Flannery arrived with prayers and words of encouragement and a bucket of Kentucky Fried Chicken. Such was the way of life in Gabriel's Crossing.

Allison alternated between Ryan's bedside and the window at the end of the hall overlooking the parking lot. Security lamps had come on, casting their stick-figure shadows onto the pavement. Jake would be in Fort Worth by now, in pain inside and out. Gone only a few hours and she missed him already.

The weeks and months ahead, especially this first Christmas she'd planned to spend with him, loomed dark and lonely.

Her mom moved toward her carrying two disposable cups, and Allison wondered how much coffee and cocoa and how many hugs and words of comfort her mother had dispensed today. "You look like you could use some cocoa."

"Thanks, Mama."

"Are you okay? You're very quiet."

Allison accepted the small cup and let the warmth spread into her cold fingers. She felt cold all over today, like a blast of winter inside her soul. "A lot on my mind."

"You want to talk about him? Or about the confrontation with Quinn?"

Mom's soft, accepting tone opened the door to spill out her sorrow, but instead she said, "No use talking. The boys finally got what they wanted. Jake's gone."

Tears pushed up in her throat. She swallowed them down but not before her mother noticed.

Karen set her cup on the window ledge and stroked her daughter's hair away from her face the way she'd done for as long as Allison could remember. A gentle stroke of comfort and caring that only a mother could give.

Had Jake's mother ever done that for him?

"I'm sorry, sweetheart." Mama didn't say the obvious. She had warned Allison that Jake would hurt her.

"Jake never had this."

Her mother cocked her head to one side. "Never had cocoa?"

Allison managed a smile. "He didn't have someone like you, a mother to stroke his hair and bring him cocoa when life stunk."

"Pat did her best and was good to him, but he was a lonely child. The way he tagged along with you kids tugged at my heartstrings."

Always on the outside, always alone. "Mine, too. You were good to him."

"I never minded an extra place at the table."

"I love him, Mama. I think I've loved him forever."

Her mother looked at her with a mix of sorrow and understanding. "I know, and my heart breaks to see you hurt. And don't try to deny it because I know you, Allison. Those soft brown eyes are like a puppy's. They reveal every emotion. You're hurting badly."

The tears she'd kept at bay leaped to the fore. Allison batted her eyes and turned toward the window. Beyond the hospital, a Buchanon-built housing addition glowed with the multicolored promise of Christmas.

Her mother tenderly rubbed a hand between her daughter's shoulders.

"I wanted to go with him." Allison batted her eyes, fighting the blur.

"Oh, honey."

"He wouldn't let me. He said I'd hate him someday if he took me away from all of you."

"He was right."

"How can this be right? I love him. He loves me. Nothing's right about any of this!"

Before her mother could respond, Dad's voice called to them from the door to Ryan's room.

Mom's hand spasmed on Allison's back. Allison spun around.

Her dad motioned. "Come on. Hurry."

The women exchanged looks. Fear streaked up Allison's back. "Is Ryan—"

A smile broke over her father's face. "He's awake."

Relief, like a warm flood, caused her shoulders to sag, but she quickly recovered and followed her mother down the hallway.

Inside the room, Buchanon bodies made a rectangle around the hospital bed. Allison pushed in between Quinn and Jayla.

Tears streamed down her sisters' faces at the sight of Ryan with his eyes open staring around at his relatives.

"I'm thirsty."

Charity stuck a yellow plastic straw to her son's lips. "How's your head, baby?"

"It hurts. What happened?"

"You got hurt by a bull. Don't you remember?"

His gaze fell to the white sheets. "Yeah. Is Chet okay?"

"He's fine. You were the one Jake put on the bull."

His head came up. "Huh?"

The adults exchanged glances, worried about Ryan's memory glitch. "Jake Hamilton, the one who was teaching you how to ride. He helped you get on the bull. Don't you remember?"

Eyes wide now, Ryan moved his head slowly from side to side. "Jake wasn't there."

"Yes, baby. You've hurt your head a little. The headache is preventing you from remembering."

"No, Mom, Jake wasn't there. He would have been mad

if he'd seen us there again. He told us never to go near the bulls."

Charity's hand went to her mouth. "Chet said Jake was teaching you, that he helped you on."

"But that's not true!" As if he realized he'd said too much, Ryan stopped talking and slid deeper into the bed, his eyes squeezed shut.

A silent moment of realization hummed on the hospital-scented air before Quinn ground out, "Get Chet in here. Now."

"Whoa, whoa, this is not the place." Dawson hitched his chin toward the door. "Let's take this conversation outside."

Mom and Charity stayed behind but the rest filed out into the hall to talk to Chet. When he heard the news that Ryan would be all right, tears formed in his eyes.

"Want to tell us what really happened out there today, Chet?" Brady asked gently as he went down on one knee beside the boy's chair. "Ryan says Jake warned you away from the bulls."

Chet hung his head. "Yeah. He did."

"Chet!" The boy's mother paled.

Allison put a hand on the woman's shoulder. "Tell us the truth, Chet. It's wrong to blame someone else. What happened?"

In a mumble with his chin low on his chest, Chet told the story of sneaking off to play rodeo cowboy. "Ryan went first, and then he fell and he couldn't get up and—" his lips trembled "—Jake saw us. He yelled for us to get away. And when Ryan fell, Jake ran inside the pen. He threw himself in front of the bull so it wouldn't horn Ryan anymore. Jake got knocked down. I thought for a minute he was dead, too." Two tears rolled down his cheeks and dripped on his jeans. "I thought they were both dead, but

Jake got up and made the bull chase him. He was trying to save Ryan. Ryan was bleeding and—"

Brady patted Chet's knee. "I think we understand now. You don't have to say any more."

For a moment, quiet reigned in the small waiting area, as they each absorbed the news. Jake, the Jake they despised, had saved Ryan's life.

Allison's pulse hammered against her temples. Chet had lied. And the Buchanons had accepted the lie as easily as breathing because it implicated Jake.

"Is that why the two of you were brawling like Neanderthals in the waiting room? Because Chet told a lie to keep himself out of trouble?" She pointed a finger around the box of Buchanons, her voice rising. "And you *all* believed a little boy over a grown man? The man who saved Ryan's life!"

"Now, Allison," Jayla said. "This is no place for drama. Nobody likes Jake anyway."

The revelation was the final straw. She couldn't bear it any longer. Allison burst into tears.

"Whoa. Wait. Don't do that." Quinn patted her shoulder and looked completely out of his element. "Somebody make her stop. Allison doesn't cry."

"You. You mean-spirited, unforgiving cretins." She glared at the other stunned faces. "All of you. You claim to be Christians, but you don't have an ounce of forgiveness in your souls. You want grace for yourselves but you refuse to extend it to a man who's done everything he can to make up for hurting Quinn. You stubbornly refuse to believe anything good about him, and he's a good man. A man I love. And he loves me. So much that he left town rather than come between me and my family. What does that tell you about yourselves and him? Huh? Answer me that?"

She was so upset, she didn't quite comprehend all the words streaming from her mouth. The Jake she knew tumbled out and suddenly she didn't care about her humiliation or the secret she'd kept for years.

"I never told you because I was afraid. You had enough on your plate, according to Jake. You didn't need anything else to worry about. But he was there for me the night a boy tried to rape me."

Brady leaped to his feet. "Who?"

"Doesn't matter now, and I won't ever tell you. The point is Jake stopped him. He fought for me and got a busted nose for his efforts. And like the gentleman he is, he carried me to his truck and took care of me. Not once did he ever criticize me or make me feel less than a good person because I'd been stupid enough to go off alone with…that boy."

Brady's face reflected that of his brothers in a mix of horror and shock. "We never knew. How could we not know?"

"I didn't want you to know. I was afraid of what you might do, of the trouble you might get into if you knew. But Jake Hamilton is not the villain you've made him out to be. He made a horrible mistake nine years ago, but he's made up for it a thousand times over. First with me that awful night on the river. Today with Ryan."

When she finished, the group was as silent as an empty church. Shocked faces stared back at her, some ashamed, others suddenly aware of their collective misjudgment.

"Wow, sis," Sawyer said. "You're something when you're all fired up."

"Jake thinks I'm something all the time." But now, she was nothing but drained dry. "I never meant to tell you, but I'm so tired of Jake being the bad guy."

Dawson's face was a picture of remorse. "When Quinn

was injured at Jake's hand, all of us, but especially Quinn lost something we valued greatly. Maybe too much. In our pain and loss, we forgot what Jesus taught about forgiveness."

"We didn't forget," Brady said. "We ignored it."

"We hurt, so we hit back. It didn't seem like such a big sin. To despise one person who'd caused us grief. But I see now, we not only hurt Jake, we hurt our little sister. We hurt ourselves."

Quinn massaged his right biceps, voice distant and thoughtful. "I've hated Jake Hamilton for so long, I forgot what a good friend he used to be."

"He was. He still is. He loves all of you." Allison sniffed, wiping at her eyes with her sweater sleeve. "Do you know what he said to me, Quinn? He said you had a right to hit him all you wanted. He would let you. You could pound him into the earth and he wouldn't fight back."

"Ah, man." Quinn rubbed a hand over his eyes. "You all know Jake wasn't the only one drinking beer that day. But we let him take all the blame."

"Yeah." A chorus of agreement passed between the brothers.

Quinn touched Allison's shoulder. "You really love the guy, little sis?"

Her lips began to tremble. "With all my heart."

"I think I speak for everyone when I say, go get him. We need to have a heart-to-heart. This time without threats."

A glance at the other faces confirmed Quinn's statement, but Allison shook her head. "I can't. He's gone." The tears flooded in again. She swallowed, the knot thick in her throat. "And even if he was still in Gabriel's Crossing, he'd never believe the Buchanon brothers would forgive him."

"Gone doesn't mean anything these days. The roads run in every direction. Where is he?"

"Fort Worth. The rodeo. He needed to make some money."

Quinn glanced at Brady. "You thinking what I'm thinking?"

"It's a long drive."

"Then we better get started."

Behind the chutes, Jake leaned against the far wall, dejected. He'd lasted less than two seconds before his side gave out and the Badlands bull slammed him to the ground. He shouldn't have tried to ride after everything that happened today. His head wasn't in it.

Now his wallet was thinner than ever, but the sale of the bulls would pay off Granny Pat's house and tide him over until he could find a regular job.

"Tough break, Hamilton," another cowboy called as he passed by.

"Yeah." He rubbed a tired hand down his face. Might as well head for the truck. The cab would be his bed for the night and he was bone weary and sorer than he wanted to be. He'd laid off too long.

The trouble was his heart wasn't in bull riding anymore either.

He missed Allison. He missed Granny Pat. He missed his friends, his bulls, his hometown. Not everyone there hated him.

He ambled back to the locker room to collect his gear, thinking as he went.

Granny Pat's words kept coming back to him. Did she really think he was running away like his mother had?

Praying in his heart for guidance, he took his belongings from a locker, slammed the metal door and started back out into corridor.

He could move his trailer back to Gabriel's Crossing.

Or maybe sell it and move in with his grandma. The paper mill might hire him. He wasn't afraid of hard work and in a few years he could rebuild his herd.

Nah, none of that made sense. The problems would still be there.

So would Allison.

He wasn't sure if he could keep going without her. The temptation to bring her along had ripped through him like a chain saw.

Jake chuffed. Or maybe that was the bruise on his side.

With his navy blue duffel bag over one shoulder, he headed down the corridor toward the exit. Cowboys passed, nodded or spoke. The smell of the arena and animals drifted to him, as natural as sunrise.

Working in a factory wouldn't be easy. He was an outdoor man. But he'd do whatever necessary to get by.

As he approached the perpendicular hallway, four men rounded the corner. His stomach lurched. Stride for stride like old west gunslingers, the Buchanon brothers came toward him in a wall of muscle and mad. Jake stopped in his tracks. Was Ryan—?

Please no. Let the boy be all right.

But why else would the Buchanons be here?

Wary, he dusted a hand down his chaps and prepared for the news and the inevitable confrontation. He was too sore and heartsick to fight with the Buchanons tonight.

As the men came closer, their big bodies filling the corridor from side to side, he asked, "Is Ryan all right?"

Quinn spoke first. "He'll be fine. A concussion. And a confession."

Jake briefly closed his eyes. "Thank God." When he opened them again, he noticed something he'd missed before. The expressions on the Buchanon boys' faces. Not anger, but something else. "You came all this way to tell me?"

Quinn shook his head. "Partly, but we mostly came with an olive branch."

"An apology," Brady said when Jake stared at them, dumbfounded.

"I don't understand. You don't owe me an apology. I'm the one—" He bit down on his back jaw, felt the pain of Quinn's punch, the pain he deserved.

"We were wrong, Jake. We've been wrong for a long time but we want to make things right."

Jake couldn't believe what he was hearing. "You do?"

"Chet told us the truth about today, and Allison told us some other things." Brady clapped Jake on the shoulder. "Thank you for taking care of our sister."

"I love her. I'd do anything for her." The words came out on their own, but they were true. If the Buchanons took offense, so be it.

"Even walk away?"

"I already did."

The four brothers exchanged glances.

Brady spoke up. "Well, we kind of took offense to that. You running off on our little sister. Her crying. Right here at Christmas. We thought you wanted to make her happy."

"I do. She'll move on, find someone good enough for her."

"I think she already has."

"We brought you an early Christmas present, Jake. Don't mess it up this time."

Bewildered, his heart hammering like a jackhammer, he watched as the wall of men separated and there stood his love.

"Allison." Before he could finish the thought, she launched across the small space like a linebacker after the sack, and into Jake's arms.

His duffel and bull rope fell with a thud as he caught

her, holding on for dear life, hardly able to believe this was happening. Afraid that any minute, he'd awaken and discover he was dreaming.

But then Quinn spoke one final time and set him free to love.

"Go on, brother, kiss her. But wait until I turn my back. I don't want to have to hit you again."

Laughing, the four brothers turned away in unison, sharing a round of high fives.

Reality slowly seeped in. They'd forgiven him. He and Allison had the Buchanon blessing. She was here.

"I can't believe this."

"Believe it. Come home."

"Tonight I knew I could never stay away forever. I'm sorry, so sorry for hurting you."

"Will you shut up and kiss her, already!" A chorus of laughs came from the wall of backs turned toward him.

Jake needed no further invitation. As the world around him righted, he lowered his face to Allison's.

And finally, after nine long years, he could breathe again.

Epilogue

The Buchanon house was a zoo on Christmas Day. With the smell of turkey and sage stuffing lingering on the air long after dinner, Jake stood in the divider between the dining and family rooms. The house was jammed with Buchanons, friends of the Buchanons, neighbors with nowhere else to go for Christmas and he and his grandmother. Miss Pat, who'd made the trip on her walker, insisted on helping with the dishes, a sight that thrilled her grandson who'd despaired of her ever functioning on her own again.

He couldn't believe the changes since that night at the rodeo. As awkward as the initial days had been, the Buchanons were a family who kept their word. He was welcomed, forgiven. Though they were no closer than before to discovering who was vandalizing Buchanon work sites, no one pointed fingers at Jake. He prayed that never changed.

Allison's laugh came to him from the kitchen and suddenly she was there, her small hands on his shoulders. "Hey, cowboy. Ready to open presents?"

"I already have the only ones I ever wanted. You." He jerked his chin toward the passel of family sprawled around the living room television. "Them. Home."

Her brown eyes softened. "Oh, Jake. This is the best Christmas ever."

"I can't argue that." Things weren't perfect. Problems remained with the mortgage and finances, but now that he was home for good, now that he had Allison at his side, he was confident something would work out.

In one corner of the large family room stood a massive Christmas tree trimmed in gold and red with a sprinkling of tiny football helmets and a lighted angel on top.

Someone flipped the television channel away from football and for once, no one complained as the sounds of the season came softly through the speakers. In a flurry of wrapping paper and ribbons, the family tore into gifts.

Jake and Allison sat on the floor in between Quinn and Jayla. Gifts piled into his lap, but his focus was Allison and her family, the hot air balloon feeling in his chest. He unwrapped a new wallet, a belt he and Allison had seen at the rodeo, a dinner for two at the Chinese restaurant. The pile grew until he was amazed.

"I can't believe this," he said, dumbfounded at what lay in the bottom of a small box.

Allison, deep in scarves and jewelry and books, looked up. "What is it?"

He handed her the card. "Did you have anything to do with this?"

As she read, Allison gasped, her expression turning from incredulity to joy. "The mortgage is paid in full."

"You didn't know?"

"No! This is wonderful. You won't have to sell your bulls. You can start your ranch."

Yes, and he could do something else, too. "But who?"

"Does it matter? This is the note, cancelled, fulfilled." Eyes dancing, she kissed the corner of his mouth. "The Hamilton debt is paid in full."

The wonder of the day overwhelmed him. "Kind of like Jesus, huh?" he said, softly. "He paid our debts when we couldn't."

"Exactly. Oh, I'm so happy for you. For us."

He caught her hand and drew it to his heart. Around them, paper flew and people talked while some kid sang about wanting a hippopotamus for Christmas. He didn't want a hippopotamus. He wanted her.

"I should have bought you a ring."

Allison froze in midchatter. "What did you say?"

"I thought we'd have to wait for years, but with the mortgage paid and the new job with Manny, we can make this work. Marry me, Allison. Be my Christmas present forever."

She opened her mouth, closed it, opened it again. Tears flowed down her cheeks.

"Don't cry. I love you." Jake's whole body quivered with the joy and hope she'd brought into his life.

Then surrounded by the awe and beauty of Christmas and the gift of family, Allison threw herself into his arms and through laughter and tears promised to be his.

And that was his best Christmas present ever.

* * * * *

*Look for more books
in* New York Times *bestselling author
Linda Goodnight's new miniseries*
THE BUCHANONS *in 2015.
You'll find them wherever
Love Inspired books are sold!*

Dear Reader,

Family is a recurring theme in all of my books, primarily because family means so much to me. In this new series, beginning with *Cowboy Under the Mistletoe,* you will meet the Buchanons, a large, close-knit family with strengths and weaknesses, failings and successes much like those of any family. I hope you've enjoyed meeting Allison and Jake and will join me in the next books when we get better acquainted with Brady, the warrior with the kind heart, and Quinn, the athlete whose golden dreams turned to ashes. Both of these wild Buchanon men need a strong woman to tame them—and I have just the ladies waiting in the wings.

I love hearing from readers. You can contact me and sign up for newsletter updates at www.lindagoodnight.com.

Until the next time, thank you and happy reading.

Merry Christmas,

Linda Goodnight

Questions for Discussion

1. Name and describe the hero and heroine in this story. Who was your favorite? To whom could you best relate?

2. Were there other characters you particularly enjoyed? Which ones and why?

3. Did you have a least favorite character? Who and why? Did you change your feelings about him/her at any point?

4. The Buchanons are important people in Gabriel's Crossing. What do they do for a living? How does their occupation add conflict to the story?

5. What happened to cause the animosity between Jake and the Buchanon brothers?

6. Do you believe a minor should be held accountable for his misdeeds? If so, to what extent? Is a teenager able to make adultlike decisions?

7. Jake suffers guilt and remorse for the teenage incident, so much so that he moved away and avoids his hometown. Do you think guilt can change the course of a person's future? How?

8. Jake suffered childhood losses. What were they? Discuss them. Do those losses still affect him as an adult? If so, how?

9. Have you or anyone you have ever known held a grudge? Was the anger justified? What does scripture say about holding grudges?

10. Allison Buchanon comes from a large, close-knit family she adores. How does this become a source of conflict for her?

11. Allison and Jake share a secret. What was it? How did it bond the pair together?

12. Describe the setting. When and where does the story occur?

13. Jake has always longed for a strong family. Discuss how this plays a role in his reasoning when he rejects Allison's bid to leave town with him.

14. Family and forgiveness are dual themes in the book. Discuss each one, how they complement and conflict with each other and how both play a role in the resolution.